CURSED
SIGHT

ALSO BY T. G. AYER

Young Adult Paranormal

THE VALKYRIE SERIES

Dead Radiance

Dead Radiance Audio

Dead Embers

Dead Embers Audio

Dead Chaos

Dead Chaos Audio

Dead Wrath

Dead Silence

Joshua - Dead Radiance

Joshua II - Dead Embers

Joshua III - Dead Chaos

Joshua IV - Dead Wrath

Joshua V - Dead Silence

THE HAND OF KALI SERIES

Fire & Shadow

Blood & Gold

Time & Fate

Fury & Virtue

Spirit & Soul

THE DARKWORLD ORIGINS

Pyros (Logan)
Ailuros (Kailin)

~

THE DARK SIGHT SERIES

Dark Sight
Cursed Sight
Vissarion
Shadow Sight
Dark Prophecy
Cursed Prophecy
Shadow Prophecy

~

THE APSARA CHRONICLES

Immortal Bound
Gods Ascendent
Dominion Falling
Vengeance Born
Last Legion

~

A SEASON OF ASH AND BONE

Heartfyre

~

Adult Sci-Fi

HANDS ASSASSIN

Death Dealer

Death Mark

Death Strike

Hand's Assassins Series

∾

NEW ADULT CONTEMPORARY THRILLER W/A TONI VALLAN

Beautiful Collision

Beautiful Conviction

∾

PSYCHOLOGICAL HORROR W/A TONI VALLAN

Dark Shadows

Splinter

CURSED SIGHT

A DARK SIGHT NOVEL #2

Cover art by Eduardo Priego

Cover art © T.G. Ayer. All rights reserved.

ISBN-13: 978-0995112605

ISBN-10: 0995112606

INFINITE
INK
BOOKS

CURSED SIGHT

USA TODAY BESTSELLING AUTHOR

T.G. AYER

CHAPTER 1

*F*or Allegra Damascus terrible visions of the future could not compare to the memories of her past.

Allegra stood in the bathroom of the aircraft, grounding her feet to compensate for the inevitable swaying and jittering of the flight. Her hands quivered and she curled them into fists, ignoring the bite of her fingernails as they dug into the soft skin of her palms.

She didn't want to look at her hands, preferred to pretend that what her eyes showed her was a lie. But—as if drawn by some kind of terrible, powerful force—she found her gaze pulled toward her shaking palms.

Palms covered in bright red blood.

Fat, glistening drops fell from her fingertips into the tiny gray, fake-marble washbasin, slipping slowly toward the drain. A dull roar emanated from the drain, as if some dark monster eagerly waited to sip at the droplets.

Allegra let out a soft whimper, then grabbed the nearest dispenser and began to squeeze soap onto her fingers. Too late, she felt her skin skid against the white liquid—hand-lotion. She let out a frustrated groan. With the heel of her palm she pressed the faucet and rubbed her fingers desperately beneath the thin trickle of water.

Blood won't come out with lotion, an amused voice whispered in her ear.

Tears filled Allegra's eyes as she watched the water rinse away the sticky creme, only to leave her fingers still stained red.

A harsh banging on the door beside her made her flinch, eliciting a hollow shriek from her parched throat. She shifted to face the door, her body shuddering from shock and fear. Shock, she understood. The fear seemed entirely unwarranted, making Allegra wonder if she was slowly going crazy.

Was this what happened to oracles like her?

Swallowing hard, she grabbed a wad of paper towels and hurriedly dried her hands. As she opened the door, she found her path blocked by a red-faced, portly man who hovered at the door, his hand on the doorjamb.

She glared up at him, much more composed now than she had been a few minutes earlier. Thankfully. "Excuse me," she said, pointedly glancing at his hand which still blocked her exit.

"Excuse me? That's all you have to say after holding me up for so long?" He spat the words at her, taking an intimidating step toward her, crowding into her personal space and forcing her to step back inside the washroom.

His accent was so thick—something from the Amazonian continent, she was sure—Allegra found she had to concentrate on his intonations in order to understand his words.

Over the last few weeks of her life, Allegra had been reduced to many things she'd never imagined were possible. And now, as she stood before this overweight, overbearing excuse for a man, she acknowledged she was also a killer.

She blinked as the man smirked and lowered his hand, bringing his elbow level with her shoulder, effectively blocking her from leaving. The idiot was preventing her from doing exactly what he demanded she do.

Without thinking, Allegra lifted her hand, and grabbed hold of his wrist. She would have pushed him away. Should have pushed him away, especially when the galley and the narrow aisle in the aircraft began to fade away.

Instead, she held on tightly as her vision filled with the sight of a small city, a modern mix of old pueblo homes, iron-roofed shacks and ancient stone pyramids.

The city flowed down the side of the mountain like a waterfall of human detritus, both a sign of the ravaged earth as well as proof that some had prospered while most had crawled out from insignificance on the strength of body and broken fingernails.

But as Allegra watched, the city shifted, moving, as if turned into a lake of molten lava, undulating and then sliding down the mountainside.

A blast of heat slammed into Allegra, and she gasped as the face of the mountain split in two and a gigantic chasm opened up, a strange green glow seeping through. The crack tore through the hillside as if some sadistic giant held each end, intent on ripping it in two.

And then the buildings began to shift, not down to the valley but over the edge into the blackness of the dark cavern, into the depths of nothing.

Warm fingers gripped her hand and from the tingle of electricity against her flesh, Allegra knew they belonged to Max. The contact of his skin broke the hold of the vision and the scene—so filled with death and destruction—began to fade away.

She blinked and looked around her, praying she hadn't made a scene. Max lowered his head and bowed, releasing her hand discretely. "My Lady? Could I be of assistance?"

The passenger blinked at Max's respectful tone and the man's hand dropped a fraction.

Allegra's eyes narrowed as she stared at Max, "I'm fully capable of dealing with him, Commander."

Another blink from the man who seemed more impressed at Max's 'Commander' than Allegra's 'Lady'.

The man took a step back, bumping into the flight attendant behind him. The woman forced a smile onto her face and peered around the man, her gaze meeting Allegra and Max.

In a blink she was bowing. "My Lady. How may I be of service?" She raised her head slightly to meet Allegra's eyes.

Glancing behind the attendant Allegra watched as her harasser slid into another washroom and closed the door with a clatter. The ruddiness of his cheeks had deepened and Allegra was sure the man must have been intoxicated.

Allegra gave the girl a smile, "I'm quite fine . . ." she tipped her head to read her name tag, ". . . Keren."

Keren bobbed her blonde head, though she was still frowning as she glanced over her shoulder at the toilet door, "Are you sure I shouldn't be putting him in lockup until landing?"

Allegra shook her head. "I don't believe so. Not unless he gets any more drunk than he already is."

Keren smiled, although the emotion did not reach her eyes. It was all too clear the passenger's behavior toward the Pythia had worried the girl.

"I'm fine, really. And thank you for your concern." With a soft smile, Allegra shifted toward Max who stood aside at the end of the aisle, waiting for her like a guard dog.

She shouldn't complain considering he'd proved on many an occasion how much she needed him.

Needed his protection.

Not him.

Allegra straightened her shoulders and headed past Max to their cabin. Max had attempted to obtain private seating to maintain Allegra's privacy, but the FAPA travel coordinator had issued them with business class allocations.

Thankfully, Allegra's reputation had preceded her and as soon as the pilot had discovered *she* was a passenger he'd insisted on settling her in the deluxe cabin, a small six-seater private room at the front of the plane reserved for royalty and the super-rich.

And apparently now for Pythias too.

Max opened the gleaming mahogany door and ushered her inside, then shut it with an angry click.

"Was that necessary?" he asked, keeping his voice low. He leaned over a little, always conscious of his height with the low ceiling of the plane's interior.

"What?" she asked, navigating across the cabin to a window seat, and sinking onto the soft custard-colored leather of the armchair.

"Your excursion across to the business class lavatory. That was not out of necessity."

Allegra turned and stared at Max, a defiant thrust to her chin. "I was suffocated in here . . . I needed space. So, I went for a walk." And suddenly her anger faded and she found herself shifting her eyes away from his intense gaze. She faced the window and stared out at the clouds, "I just needed to be alone and . . . Well . . ."

Max took the seat beside her. "I know you feel claustrophobic. These flights are long. But we don't have a security contingent any longer. You do have to be careful."

Allegra bit her lip, swallowing the words threatening to spill from her lips. She was so very tired.

She ignored Max and leaned her forehead against the cool glass, staring out at the clouds gathered so close to the plane you would have been forgiven for thinking the aircraft was sitting upon the clouds the way the gods were once said to have lived— way above the mortal world, watching over humanity from a distance.

Allegra indulged in the vision, hoping it would distract her from the slight tremor in her fingers, from the copper aroma filling her nostrils.

Max's voice rang in her ears. Not his words, just his voice, the low baritone a sexy rumble that reverberated within the pit of her stomach.

He'd meant well, with his calming words designed to set her at ease, to coax to her the way a horse-trainer would seduce a wild filly and bring her to heel.

But though he'd meant to bring her to a state of calm, he'd failed. Maximus Vissarion still believed his words were sufficient to have an effect on her.

They weren't.

Allegra inhaled softly, taking the air deep into her lungs, all while ensuring the sound remained as silent as possible. Beside her somewhere, within a mere few feet, Max would be sitting, watching her with his keen eyes, worry lines creasing his brow.

He worried still, believing his concern meant something.

It didn't.

But perhaps she was being unfair. He could still be concerned, could still worry. And perhaps those emotions were genuine enough. The only problem was those feeling mattered little to her now.

A few weeks ago, his concern would have set her heart aflutter, would have stirred her blood to heat. But now, knowing whatever they'd had between them had been a lie, Allegra merely felt tainted.

Under order of General Aulus, FAPA Commander Vissarion had attempted to seduce Allegra, all in the hopes of ensuring her powers, her ability to foretell the future, would remain within the control of the New Germanic States, providing her birth country with a supremely unfair advantage over the rest of the world.

In addition, such an advantage was illegal according to the Treaty of the Oracle of Pythia.

Allegra had since learned the Treaty of Pythia essentially gave her the key to the world, access to all countries without restriction of movement. It also gave the world access to her power.

The powers of the Pythia belonged to all.

Max's betrayal—or rather, Allegra's discovery of that betrayal

—had struck deep, having come so close on the heels of her own failure.

Corina Brava had died in Allegra's arms, and nothing could ever change the fact that had Allegra been smarter, or more proactive, or braver, she could have saved the seer.

Their last mission to Bharat in the Indus Continent to eliminate a deadly virus had ended in success. The population of the world was safe, billions of people waking up in the morning and going about their day, with not a single inkling of the life lost to save them.

What was an unknown hero worth when the threat remained unknown too? Corina's sacrifice was invisible, much like the stain of her blood on Allegra's hands.

Allegra shifted, her body beginning to grow stiff again. Her leather-clad legs stretched out in front of her, and Allegra gave a half smile. She'd taken up wearing the pants after being unable to return the clothing the seer had lent her while in London two weeks ago.

She wore a white overdress, split up the front to her waist. The style was a statement in itself, thumbing her nose at the unfeminine leather by pairing it with a Roman-style white silk dress.

She'd earned a few strange looks but being the Pythia, she believed she'd begin a trend before too long. How Xenia would laugh should it come to pass. Her best friend was the trendsetter, the daring fashionista with a taste for bright colors and eclectic garments.

She would approve.

Xenia had not been impressed when Allegra had called her from Athens to say she wouldn't be coming home just yet. Allegra's side-trip to Peru had not gone down well, but she'd soothed her frantic friend and had promised to call and keep her posted.

Allegra let out another sigh, then stiffened, waiting for Max's voice as he asked if she was alright.

But only a soft snore drifted toward her.

She sighed again, and folded her blood-stained fingers on her lap as she turned her attention again to the land of clouds outside the window.

Maybe she could find a hint of peace somewhere within the beautiful sky.

CHAPTER 2

The sound of snoring snapped Max to wakefulness so sharply that the bones in his neck gave a soft crack. He blinked, his gaze landing on Allegra's booted feet, and he tracked her long shapely limbs up to the curve of her waist.

Her eyes were closed as she leaned against the glass, and she seemed at peace. But Max feared that perhaps her moments of unconsciousness were the only times she was untroubled. He sent up a silent prayer—to whom he was not entirely sure—in the hopes that her dreams remained untouched.

Sadly though, he suspected they wouldn't be. She'd been through so much. More especially at the hands of Lord Severus Langcourt. The report had arrived just before they'd left Athens.

The tunnels in which Pienius and Max's team had found Allegra were beneath the sprawling lands of Lord Langcourt. It had only taken a short while to make their way through the conveniently collapsed tunnels in order to access the villa.

Langcourt had escaped and had left his family home in ruins, setting off explosions all around the property that had resulted in at least a dozen deaths.

Now the man had disappeared into thin air, and despite an internationally coordinated effort, was nowhere to be found.

After her experience of torture at the sadistic man's hands, Max had expected Allegra to suffer some form of post-traumatic stress but she hadn't.

Max had been grateful, glad she wouldn't carry that burden with her for years to come. But as relieved as he was that Langcourt's torture had failed to break Allegra's soul, he was equally heartbroken to see her in her current condition.

He'd seen this before, the shaking hands, the jittery movements, the wide-eyes filled with fear as they stared at something visible only to them. He'd seen her stare at her fingers, curl them into vicious balls, hide them within the fabric of her skirt. He'd seen the red, raw edges that spoke of excessive washing, watched her make a thousand trips to the bathroom only to wash her hands and return, squeezing them tightly again.

She suffered as a survivor, as one who should have done more, as one who had failed to save those who'd perished. He knew firsthand how that felt. Corina was his agent—had been his agent—and he'd trained her, watched over her when she'd first entered FAPA, counseled her when her seer's ability had troubled her.

Her death had hit him hard in the gut, and deep in the heart, but he'd had no time to mourn his friend, no time to assuage his own guilt at allowing the team to be put in such a position for her death to happen so easily.

Had he been distracted by the impending plague, or perhaps by his concern for the Pythia's safety? Or was it because of the personal nature of his emotional attention to Allegra?

Now he suspected her coolness with him was the best and most appropriate stance to take. She'd shut him out so swiftly it had taken him a while to zero in on what could have caused her change in behavior.

Max had his money on General Aulus.

His superior had come all the way to Delphi to insist Max saw his mission through, to ensure Max brought the Oracle back to the States. But Aulus hadn't bargained on Allegra.

Whatever she'd overheard of that conversation she certainly knew enough to believe Max had used her, had betrayed her, had meant to bed her as a means to control her.

He could still see the naked pain in her eyes when she'd told him she wanted nothing to do with him. But, despite her dismissal of him, he'd remained at her side, refusing to return with Aulus, thumbing his nose at his commanding officer's authority.

He'd fully expected to receive his dismissal papers, but days had passed as they'd made preparations to depart for Peru and there'd been no directive from Aulus to return to the Capital.

Max supposed he should acknowledge such good fortune, especially considering his luck could very well run out tomorrow.

CHAPTER 3

The city of Qusqu was like nothing Allegra had ever seen.

Giant pyramids rose into the sky, and where cities in the States were filled with Roman—and Greek—styled villas, the Incans had never adopted the vertical building structures into their architectural landscape.

As Allegra and Max descended the stairs from the aircraft, luggage in hand, they'd been met by half a dozen uniformed policemen. Their lapel badges, and the tags on their jackets, indicated they were Peruvian law enforcement as well as airport security.

One of the policewomen—who bore a few more stars and badges on her lapels than the rest—walked toward Max as he stepped off the last riser of the stairs. Allegra watched as the woman studied Max, giving his broad shoulders and height an appreciative glance.

Her midnight hair and olive skin proclaimed her Qulla heritage, and when she spoke her accent was tinged with the rounded tones of the Puquina language of the region.

She turned her attention to Allegra and met her eyes, offering her a low solemn bow. "My Lady. I am honored to meet you." Her respect was clear in her tone and bearing, although it seemed she was the only one in the contingent who possessed the same respect for Allegra's position.

The officer straightened then and turned back to Max. "Commander Vissarion," she said, saluting Max who responded in kind, giving her a curious glance. Max's salute drew a look of relief from the woman and she nodded, "I'm Chief Inspector Athena Nostrus. I apologize for accosting you in this manner but unfortunately my hands are tied. We're here to escort you to the NGS embassy until such time as your visa has been reissued, or you are required to leave Peru."

The inspector's apology was clearly reflected in her eyes and Allegra understood CI Nostrus really was performing this particular duty against her will.

Max frowned. "I was not aware that the Pythia required a visa," he said scanning the small law-enforcement contingent. The airport security officer, a dour man with features pulled tight into unruly creases within his ample face, stepped forward, holding out a letter. Max eyed the document and smiled, "But the Pythia and I are happy to await the resolution of this . . . complication, at the NGS embassy."

The airport cop still held out the document and Allegra glanced at Max. Seemingly on the same wavelength, he reached out and took the paperwork, barely giving the man a glance before meeting Allegra's gaze and giving her an apologetic smile.

Allegra wasn't often the back-seat driver type but given the circumstances she preferred Max to fight the battles, and be the bad guy if needed. When he waved her ahead, indicating she should follow CI Nostrus—who had taken a step away from the gaggle of cops toward her vehicle—Allegra complied without a backward glance at the rest of the policemen.

Allegra gave Nostrus a pleasant smile as she reached the woman's side, hiding her own annoyance at the wrinkle in her plans. Allegra had come to investigate the site of the destruction she'd seen in her visions. She couldn't afford to be stonewalled at every turn. And given that they'd barely set foot off their plane and were already having trouble, she suspected their stay in Qusqu would not be made any easier.

The inspector led them to her vehicle—a more recent model than Allegra's beat-up old Branson A Class—and opened the door. Both Max and Allegra entered quietly, neither revealing their frustration at the turn of events.

Traffic was light as Nostrus drove them to the New Germanic States Embassy and neither Max nor Allegra felt the need to engage in conversation. Allegra suspected Max would be reluctant to provide the Qusquan police with any further leverage than they currently presumed to have.

Besides, it had grown difficult to identify where the loyalties of those they came into contact with lay. Their most recent encounters with both the Brittanic police and certain elements of the Indus government had set Allegra and Max on high alert. Now, even CI Nostrus—despite her humble demeanor—could pose a danger.

Was it all due to Allegra's standing as the Oracle of Pythia? Was she now meant to wade through political intrigue and governmental conspiracy? She'd naively assumed her role in the greater scheme of things would be one of benevolent charity, one with the aim of saving humanity. And yet she seemed to repeatedly find herself at odds with the very people she was meant to help.

Allegra sighed and stared out of the window, keeping her hands out of her peripheral vision. For now they were clean, untainted, but Allegra could never trust when they would begin to shake, or when she would see them bloodied again.

The central city of Qusqu was built on mostly level ground while a group of majestic pyramids observed the valley from a mountainside at the east end. They sat above the rest of the landscape, like a group of soldiers watching over the city.

On the left of them angling away down the valley so they were not visible from the largest of the great pyramids, was a settlement. One that made Allegra's stomach harden with trepidation.

She swallowed and shifted her wrist on the seat so that it bumped against the edge of Max's palm. The contact sent a sizzling heat through Allegra and she tamped it down, refusing to listen to a body that betrayed her feelings. She steeled herself against the heat flowing through her veins and lifted her hand away, pointing at the haphazardly built town cascading down the side of the mountain; the very same one from her vision.

Max acknowledged her with a single short nod and stared at the city, lost in thought, seemingly unaffected by her touch. Oddly, Allegra found herself disappointed.

She shifted her gaze and refocused her thoughts, her hand clasped again in her lap.

Qusqu was ancient enough that modernization ought to have visibly taken over, but nothing in its construction made Allegra think the old systems had given way to the new.

The city remained as it had once been constructed, the roads and pathways running almost parallel to each other, all leading up to the main pyramid; a gigantic building that towered over the entire city, casting a shadow across most of the more minor structures.

The New Germanic States embassy building was located near enough to the giant pyramid to claim special status, yet far enough away that it was not darkened by its shadow. Allegra was not blind to the implication of how the positioning of those buildings could echo in the relationships between the local government and the NGS.

Chief Inspector Nostrus had been quiet during the drive, and

Allegra suspected the policewoman had no idea what to say that would make the situation any better.

Silence was the best choice in such situations.

Nostrus drew up at the steps of a small pyramid, the marquee above the gold-plated double doors proclaiming 'New Germanic States Embassy'. She alighted and hurried to open Allegra's door, giving a short bow as Allegra stepped onto the bottom stair. The entire building, including the steps, was constructed from uneven stone blocks, giving the structure an earthy—yet grand—air. Part of nature, and yet apart from it; both comforting and disconcerting at the same time.

"Ambassador McIvor is aware you are coming. I did my best to ensure things move as smoothly as possible." She smiled, her lips forming a thin line, revealing her discomfort with the situation. Allegra felt for her. Nostrus offered another small bow. "I apologize again for the disrespect. And for the inconvenience."

Allegra gave her a warm smile. "I hope it is resolved soon. I have something very important to do while I'm here and I do not want to have to leave without completing my task. Too many lives are at stake." She held the chief inspector's gaze, trying to figure out if the woman was really on her side.

When Nostrus gave a low nod and said, "Whatever happens I will be happy to assist you in any way." She paused for a few moments, as if hesitant to say what was on her mind. After glancing over her shoulder, she met Allegra's eyes again and said, "I would like to ensure that you do what you came here to do. I understand enough to know the Pythia does nothing lightly. So, the fact that you are here means there is a danger lurking and it would be ignorant of us to ignore the possibility. And reckless to do nothing about it."

Her unsaid words hung in the air between them: *Even if it means going against my orders.*

Allegra blinked, unsure how to take the woman's response.

She took a breath and smiled. "Thank you, Chief Inspector. I will be in touch once we know what our plans are."

Nostrus shook her head. "Please call me Athena."

Allegra smiled and was saved from having to say anything further when Max drew to a stop at her side. He shook the Inspector's—Athena's—hand and thanked her. After an exchange of cards and numbers, Max led Allegra up the stairs to the well-guarded entrance of the embassy.

A pair of armed NGS soldiers guarded the doorway, their uniforms the standard dark red with the golden New Germanic States' crest pinned on the swag of purple fabric on each of their left shoulders. The wolf and the bear, both with bared teeth were intertwined in their eternal battle, the symbol a reminder of a bloody past.

Allegra studied the building as she ascended the stairs. A terrace ran along the entire front of the pyramid at the ground floor level, seemingly hugging the side of the building before turning around the corners at both ends where two more guards now stood, both deathly still.

As they walked to the entrance, both doors swung open. A slim, tall woman stood to the side, her large blue eyes scanning first Allegra and then Max from head to foot. Something flickered in her expression when she lifted her gaze to Max's face, but it was gone so fast Allegra wondered if she'd imagined it.

The aide beckoned them to follow her, long black hair swaying at her waist as she led the way. She wore an ankle-length white dress, patterned at the hem and wide sleeves; tribal from the looks of the brightly-colored geometric designs.

Allegra noted the aide had failed to introduce herself and wondered as to the lack of hospitality her rudeness may imply.

Still, Max said nothing so Allegra didn't either.

The aide led them across a wide hall where square stone columns dotted the large, almost cavernous space. Doors along the hall on the left and right led to offices and storage rooms, with staff coming and going, the buzz of the busy embassy putting Allegra a little at ease. Without the sound of people, the ancient building would have made her feel far too claustrophobic, as if she were walking the halls of a living tomb.

Allegra took a breath and mentally crossed her fingers. She shouldn't think about tombs and death.

That would be courting trouble.

CHAPTER 4

A hundred feet into the great stonewalled hall they came to an elevator, the sight of the metal cage sending a chill through Allegra's bones. After a cacophony of clanking and whirring, the cage descended to the ground floor, the wrought-iron gates complaining loudly as they grated open.

The aide waved them inside, barely looking up to meet their eyes. Max and Allegra entered in silence, and Allegra watched as the woman looked back at him again, her lips parting as if she wanted to say something to him. In the end her mouth formed a thin line and she turned to stare at the floor numbers painted on the inside of the elevator wall.

They rode up seventeen floors in the central lift, the gears grunting and groaning, as they worked to raise and lower a bank of three metal cages.

Within the elevator, they were surrounded first by the iron cage, and then by the stone-lined shaft which gave off a dank cold, making Allegra shiver. She imagined it was not the temperature that sent the chills up and down her spine, but rather the blood once spilled within these walls. She remembered the history of the Aztecs and their violent need for the shedding of blood in order to appease their gods.

The tribes had flourished, growing strong over the years then fading away as they'd been defeated; Incans, Aztecs, Qulla and even further in history.

As they reached the ambassador's floor, Allegra blinked against the light blazing into the top of the elevator cage, then raised a hand to shield her eyes against the bright sunshine. The contrast between the dark, cold shaft within the building, and the warmth of the sunshine set Allegra a little off-kilter.

Or it could just be jet lag.

Allegra inhaled deeply and tried to force herself to remain steady. They were high up, likely close to—if not at—the top level of the pyramid. This floor was small compared to the ground level; likely only half the size. Which made sense considering the square-based pyramid's varying levels.

The elevator gates opened onto a small waiting area occupying the space directly in front of the doors. Beyond the reception area, the corridor narrowed down to the left and the right, culminating on each side in passages dominated by large windows spilling golden sunlight onto the stone floors and flooding the halls with golden light.

The building was an ancient architectural wonder.

The long bank of three elevators, with its additional housing for the pulleys and mechanical innards, divided the floor into two large offices, one of which belonged to the ambassador who had exited and was, at that moment, walking toward them.

He was a nondescript man, medium height and build, dark brown hair that Xenia would call mousy, and a thin mustache that seemed to hover above his mouth like a dark cloud.

His only defining feature was a pair of stunning blue eyes Allegra swore were the exact color of the azure seas of the Greek Isles.

McIvor's smile was a thin line as he met them beside the

reception desk. He gave their guide a dismissive nod, and the woman simply rounded the desk and seated herself.

So not a mere aide, but Secretary to the Ambassador.

The woman sat, throwing her long hair back over her shoulder as she pulled open a drawer and appeared to become extremely busy.

The ambassador greeted Allegra first, bowing low from his hips. "My Lady. I am honored to meet you."

Allegra murmured a mutual delight at the meeting and then stepped away allowing Max to speak. She wasn't usually deferential—not that her reluctance to hold conversation could be defined as deferential—but her mood made it dangerous for her to go one-on-one with the man. She might end up saying something she shouldn't. Especially considering she wasn't at her diplomatic best having just come off a twenty-eight-hour flight.

"Ambassador McIvor, I'm hoping you can help us," Max murmured as he shook the man's hand.

McIvor nodded, and held out a hand to indicate his open office door. Then he glanced at Allegra. She shook her head. The last thing she wanted was to listen to Max arguing their case. The fact that he even had to pissed her off.

McIvor looked over at his secretary who seemed to feel his gaze on her bent head. She glanced up at him as he said, "Would you please show the Pythia to her rooms?"

Standing, the woman gave a neutral smile, grabbed something from her desk drawer and nodded before rounding the table and heading to the elevators again. Allegra assumed she was required to follow the woman. As Allegra moved she noticed the look of disapproval McIvor gave his secretary, but Allegra pretended ignorance and hurried to the elevators.

The woman—who had yet to introduce herself—stood stiff-backed in utter silence as the car took them down two floors. Her heels clacked on the stone floor as she stalked out of the elevator doors to the first room on her left and deposited Allegra at the entrance.

Holding out a brass key, she said, "Have a pleasant stay." Her voice was toneless, wooden, and Allegra wondered if she was going to present more of a problem than just a bad attitude.

Allegra smiled and reached for the key. Though she made every effort to avoid touching McIvor's secretary, Allegra's fingers brushed the other woman's as the key passed hands.

Allegra blinked.

The hallway shifted, then faded away to be replaced by a small, stuffy room. At first, Allegra assumed it was a studio apartment, with kitchen, living and sleeping areas all combined into one space, but it didn't take long to recognize the squalid, almost dilapidated nature of the room.

A bare mattress sat against the left wall, but Allegra's gaze was repelled from it, as if something was stopping her from seeing it. She focused instead beyond the bed on a short garment rail—a makeshift closet within the shack.

Water dripped from rusted spots in the metal roof, sliding in from a few gaps where two pieces of aluminum sheeting had been overlapped. Water gathered on the narrow metal lip, and had rusted up to a handspan of the metal, but the owner of the room had—instead of fixing the cause—focused only on dealing with the resulting problem.

Receptacles—a purple plastic and broken-rimmed bucket, a large metal mixing bowl, a cardboard box lined with thick wrapping plastic, a stew pot and a glass water jug—littered the floor. The sound of the droplets hitting plastic in flat thuds and then alternating with high-pitched metallic clangs, filled the room with its discordant music.

Allegra sucked in a breath, trying hard to pull herself free from the vision, but it refused to let her go. Instead, more sounds filtered through to her, and she began to register the smells around her.

Somewhere nearby a wood fire burned, although Allegra could not see the source within the room. A kerosene lamp sat in the middle of a kitchen table, but it was unlit, it's glass covering stained with soot. The walls of the room were a motley combination of metal sheeting, card-board remnants and cut off pieces of car-doors, boxes, wood pallets and even a piece of glass haphazardly taped over to cover a multitude of cracks.

The kitchen was comprised of a single hotplate while a bowl and a jug of water masqueraded as a sink and tap. A decrepit sofa sat a foot away, its seats sunken so deep it sat barely a few inches from the floor. Beneath her feet, Allegra recognized the light brown compacted sand and understood she was still within Qusqu.

Turning her attention to the bed, Allegra now understood why she'd been so reluctant to look at it. Perhaps something in her intuition had told her what she'd see.

The body of a woman lay there, her limbs splayed, her torso bathed in blood. Her shell-pink bra and panties were so soaked with blood Allegra could not differentiate between her skin and her lingerie.

The woman's neck was barely discernible beneath the caked blood, but Allegra managed to make out the jagged slash, the gory opening that revealed raw flesh, torn muscle, and ragged tendons.

Allegra would have been able to identify the women had it not been for the state of her face; battered and bruised and so swollen her features were no longer recognizable.

But Allegra knew her.

Sucking in a deep breath, Allegra let go of the secretary's hand and took a step back so far she ended up bumping into the door at her back.

The secretary's eyes widened at Allegra's reaction and then narrowed as she stared at Allegra for a little too long. Then she took a step away, her lip curling in an expression that to Allegra looked a lot like disgust.

What?

The ambassador's secretary stalked away, her dark hair swaying as she walked off. She paused at the elevator and punched the call button, then glanced over her shoulder. She met

Allegra's eyes for a long moment, the darkness in her expression sending a cold shiver down Allegra's spine.

Had it not been for her unusual dress, Allegra would not have recognized her so quickly. In her mind's eye, Allegra saw the hovel again, saw the garment rail again.

She saw the long white dress sitting on a wooden hanger, its wide skirt patterned at the hem with multicolored Aztec designs.

The elevator pinged, pulling Allegra free from the memory and she caught a flash of the secretary's skirt as she disappeared into the cage—white fabric and multicolored Aztec designs.

The ambassador's secretary was going to die a horrible death.

CHAPTER 5

*M*ax followed Ambassador McIvor inside his office and studied the man as he rounded his desk and took a seat.

He was a man who could easily get lost in a crowd, his features unremarkable, his posture unimpressive. His shoulders were broad, but he didn't seem to be a man who spent time in a gym. He could have been muscular, but in reality, he was going to be fat.

His dark brown hair was thinning on top, and his mustache was a slim line, cutting his upper lip in half a little too harshly.

Max took the seat McIvor waved at, although Max would have preferred to stand after the long flight. As he sat, he studied the unusual desk before him. It seemed to be carved from a single piece of wood, a white-gray blend that made Max wonder.

McIvor cleared his throat. "I know what you're thinking." He let out a soft laugh, his teeth glinting in the stream of sunshine flooding the office from the wide windows. "This desk is made of bukic wood. And yes, I know it's extinct, but it was a welcome gift from a local tribe. One I was unable to refuse. My superiors in the States approved my decision to keep it if it ensured the tribe's cooperation."

Max smiled. "I was not going to criticize, Ambassador."

McIvor shrugged. "I've heard it before, so perhaps I may be a little too sensitive on the matter. It's best to get these things out of the way at the start, don't you think?" When Max nodded, he continued, "So I have to express my disappointment with the way things have been handled. This whole debacle came as much of a shock to me as it must have to you."

"It has. We are curious as to how it happened and why."

"We had a call from a Qusquan diplomat returning home from a treaty discussion. He claims to have had a run-in with the Pythia which led to questions as to what she is doing here."

Max nodded. "As you can understand, the Pythia is meant to have global access."

"It's exactly what I said, but from what the Qusquan and other Amazonian countries' representatives have said, her alignment with the NGS is the crux of the problem."

"You mean me?"

McIvor smiled. "Probably not you specifically, but the fact that she's consulting for the NGS does pose what they have described as 'a conflict of interest', which I am sure you can also understand."

Max sat back, a little astounded and yet still understanding their point of view. When he'd attended Aurelia, he hadn't been the only representative in her orbit. She'd had delegates from around the world at her side almost daily, and he could see where his being her sole advisor could be seen as alignment with the NGS.

He nodded. "I can understand that. I've only been within her advisory team to bring her up to speed on things because I'd had previous experience with the Pythia Aurelia. I don't believe the Pythia Allegra would be opposed to bringing on another representative of the Amazonian continent."

McIvor nodded. "Has this been approved by the President?" The man's eyes narrowed, criticism gleaming from them.

Max paused wondering if the question was a test. He wondered too whose side McIvor came down on. Max let out a soft laugh and leaned forward. "I don't believe the Pythia has to answer to anyone. For all intents and purposes, I am in *her* employ. I'm not sure the President of the NGS has any say at all in who is seconded to the Pythia in a diplomatic capacity."

The ambassador's features tightened, and he went a few shades paler. It seemed his question had burst out without his realization of its ramifications because he now looked uncomfortable.

"Commander, I don't want you to think I'm the sort of man who will break the rules. I just thought that—given that you do report to the NGS—you'd require the President's approval."

Max gave the man a neutral smile. "Not where it concerns the Pythia and the decisions she makes. Those are her own. As is where she wishes to travel."

McIvor nodded, his spine stiff as he faced Max. "Right. That brings me back to the main point of issue here. The delegates from the continent wish to be apprised of the reason for the Pythia's visit."

"Ah. I see. They want to know what she's seen and if her visions may have ramifications that will impact them." Max got to his feet at last, unable to endure the confines of the chair any longer. "Yes, I can understand their point of view, but can you explain to them that her visit here is only a matter of checking on something? Many of her visions are like mist in the wind. They come and go, and because time is so fluid and things can change so suddenly, it can happen that a vision never comes to pass. For that reason, the Pythia would not want to alert every person, country or institution of every vision she has. It would be foolhardy to terrify people when there is no real certainty."

"I was under the impression she'd tracked that plague across the world before she put an end to it." The man was almost smirking as he sat back, watching Max intently.

"You are correct, but what's not widely known is fate and the Pythia's visions are constantly changing. Chasing that plague . . . she had to test her visions almost every day in order to keep track of it simply because people worldwide were changing their normal patterns of behaviors as they were made aware of the dangers. Imagine if we'd made international announcements that the plague originated in chickens? International mass extermination of poultry? What would that have achieved?

"Apart from the constantly changing nature of Fate, we had to be sensitive to the nature of humanity, hysterical or otherwise." Max smiled, and the ambassador returned it, but the man's expression was devoid of all mirth.

"So, I am to tell the delegation that the Pythia is investigating a . . . possible issue, but has nothing concrete yet to discuss?"

Max nodded. "You are also welcome to tell them to choose a delegate to be attached to the Pythia's team."

"Ah, yes. I am sure that will appease." He got to his feet. "Sadly, my hands are pretty much tied. I'm at the mercy of both my superiors and the Qusquan government, and I can't afford an international incident."

Max stifled a yawn. He'd already turned and headed for the door when McIvor's voice stopped him.

"Commander, there is someone else who wishes a word, if you wouldn't mind."

Max turned on his heel, hiding his frustration. "Very well. As long as it can help clear things up as soon as possible."

"Good I've arranged for the car to wait for us downstairs."

TWENTY MINUTES LATER, Max was ushered into the shaded interior of a second pyramid along the main road, this one appearing more governmental and official than the NGS embassy.

Uniformed guards and staff hurried around. One end of the ground level appeared to be a waiting room with a combination of lines and seats snaking across the floor.

Max remained silent until they were ushered up three levels where they were directed to stone-carved chairs in a sunny waiting area. He took a seat and leaned back as McIvor sat beside him. In the car, the ambassador had revealed he was meeting the Secretary of Internal Security, General Sinchi Qhapaq, which made Max wonder what was really going on.

Max sat with his head resting against the wall behind him, struggling to stay awake. McIvor wasn't exactly the engaging type when it came to conversation, and his questions seemed to all aim at one thing: to find out what the Pythia was doing in Qusqu.

After an hour of waiting, the general's aide hurried over with a note for McIvor.

"What is it?" Max asked.

The ambassador's face darkened, his ears flushing pink, which Max was unable to identify as a result of anger or fear. "He's refusing to see us."

"I thought he'd requested the visit?" Max was beginning to lose patience.

McIvor got to his feet. "He's clearly changed his mind."

Frowning, Max surged to his feet, his frustration almost at boiling point. They'd been put through so much red tape and bullshit since they'd arrived that he was beginning to feel like there was more than a mere dispute over the Pythia's relationship with the NGS.

He managed to bite his tongue, following a silent McIvor to the car.

"I'm sorry. I had thought he'd see us."

"Does he do this often?"

"What?" McIvor seemed distracted.

"Break engagements without warning."

McIvor's smile was thin and almost angry. "Qhapaq is master

of his domain. And Qusqu is his domain. He does what he wants. Who am I to say anything? Besides, I need his cooperation, so I have to be on my best behavior with him. I work on behalf of the NGS after all."

Max nodded, understanding the man's position perhaps too well.

The drive back was short, and Max hadn't been able to shrug off his irritation. He'd begun to feel like that wait had been a strategic ploy. A way to impress upon the Pythia as to who was in charge here in Qusqu.

Qhapaq seemed to like games, which in turn made Max suspect the general could be behind the visa problems.

What was Qhapaq's end-game? Max had a feeling it was nothing good.

CHAPTER 6

*W*hile Max was busy with the ambassador, Allegra had requested a car to the nearest good restaurant. According to the ambassador's secretary, a few blocks down from the NGS Embassy was a restaurant famous throughout the world for its seared chicken and blood cakes.

She could have ordered a meal and a drink in her room, but she'd wanted the sun and the bustling of people around her. Like white noise, it kept her mind a little at ease.

Besides, if they had to go home in the morning, at least she'd have seen something of this beautiful city.

She sat on a stone-paved patio, watching the sunlight sparkle off the surface of a pool so blue you'd be forgiven for thinking it was a mirror merely reflecting the clear skies above.

To think Allegra had at one time not believed in gods. It all seemed so preposterous right now. Understandable perhaps, yet so stupid.

When Max had accosted her on the beach in front of her house, accusing her of being some prophetess, she'd thought him mad. Until, of course, Xales had appeared.

A gigantic black boar, for Apollo's sake. It had snorted and pawed the ground, eyeing Max as if it had intended to tear the fragile man to pieces. Thankfully, and a little too conveniently for Allegra's liking, it had turned out Max was already acquainted with said gigantic beast.

And Max had lived.

He had spent a few days working on convincing Allegra of who and what she really was. It shouldn't have been hard to assimilate, though for Allegra it had been.

Despite the sight of the Seer's Boar, she had still found it difficult to process, thereby frustrating Commander Vissarion's most ardent efforts.

Fortunately for Allegra, and no doubt for Max too, it was the attempt on her life by Neptune, God of Oceans, that had brought her to her senses. And perhaps the fact that Xales had saved both her and her friend Xenia's lives.

Neptune had tried to kill Allegra.

She still had to take a moment to process it all.

How many women could lay claim to that statement?

Allegra sighed. It was no joke. To be brutally honest, the memory, and the reality it highlighted, terrified her. Not that it was something she could run from, either.

But, at least one of the pantheon of gods was on her side.

Apollo.

Allegra had grown up listening to her father Aleks take the god's name in vain in various ways. He'd both cursed and thanked beings who he'd thought were mere mythical figures; throwbacks from a past filled with old wives' tales and superstition.

Her father had died never knowing that every one of his curses had likely been heard. Her poor father would have been mortified. And even now Allegra still felt a little ashamed on his behalf.

She too had used Apollo's name all the time, never thinking for one moment he'd be real. She'd even prayed to him for help without believing for a single moment he'd hear her, or that he'd answer.

That in itself was a contradiction of gigantic proportions. One Allegra preferred to avoid considering, mostly because it would lead to a far too intimate investigation of her philosophical and moral beliefs.

Perhaps whatever she thought and felt didn't really mean much considering her point of view within the present moment.

She believed in Apollo.

He'd saved her from a horrible torture, coming to her aid in both physical and mystical forms. No surprise when Apollo was the patron god of the Oracle of Pythia. It was probably his duty to look after her.

Or so she hoped.

But despite her shock at Neptune's attempt on her life, Allegra hadn't really believed it until she'd met Apollo in the flesh. Then and only then, did she accept that a god—a real live murderous god—had wanted her dead.

Ever since then she'd remained wary on the water, keeping a cold eye on waves she would once have dived into without hesitation. Now she shifted in her seat and stared out at the glimmering waters of the swimming pool.

ALLEGRA TILTED HER HEAD, ensuring the wide brim of her hat hid her features. In Qusqu, she was determined to remain within the blissful peace of anonymity. Even to the point of smiling brightly at the snippy waiter who'd been so reluctant to provide her with a patio table.

The bark of a dog drew Allegra's gaze across the breadth of the pool and her heart gave a little expectant jump. But Pepper—adorable retriever and permanent companion to Allegra's best friend in all the world Xenia Silanyo—was on another continent entirely. She'd called Xenia from the plane, giving her anxious friend the details of her Amazonian stop. The last thing Allegra needed was for Xenia to worry about her.

After the attack of the sea god, and Allegra's abduction and torture not too long ago, Xenia had gone from mild-mannered and frivolous to serious and motherly.

Allegra didn't like the transformation one bit. She wanted the old Xenia back, wanted her nonsensical gossip and afternoons of on-deck cocktails while sunbathing and praying not to fall asleep while tipsy.

The dog barked again, this time the sound a little more excited and a little more familiar. When the high yipping was followed closely by crystalline laughter, Allegra straightened and pulled off her sunglasses, scanning the poolside more intently now.

She knew that laugh.

Xenia strode across the flagstone tiles with the little retriever trotting at her ankles, the skirt of her plum-colored dress flowing behind her, tossed in her wake by an errant breeze. Xenia's golden-brown skin gleamed in the heat of the Amazonian sunshine, and heads turned to follow in her wake. Xenia knew how to draw a crowd.

Exactly what Allegra did not need.

Allegra's excitement at seeing her friend overshadowed her trepidation at being recognized. She got to her feet, slid the glasses back up her nose and opened her arms. Xenia made an odd high-pitched squealing sound as she squeezed Allegra so tightly that Allegra was sure she would have burst had she not been released in time.

After returning the hug, Allegra sank to the ground and cuddled Pepper. She'd never been overly fond of dogs, but the sight of Xenia's baby, emaciated and dying as he searched the streets of a deserted water-front for food, had opened her heart to the creature. Pepper seemed to understand her change in affection, and enjoyed every second of the cuddles and scratching she provided.

"Pepper get down. Leave her alone for a bit." Xenia was laughing as she patted the dog on his head and then gently shoved him aside. "I need time with my bestie first."

Allegra laughed. "You're competing with a dog for my attention?"

Xenia chuckled. "I'm competing with the world for your attention." She tilted her head and studied Allegra. "I like the disguise."

Allegra shrugged, feeling the warmth of the sun on her skin. The strappy sundress she wore had arrived courtesy of the Ambassador's wife, and she'd been grateful. Although she'd done a little shopping in Athens, she'd not had sufficient time—with abductions and plague-chases across the world—for attending to her wardrobe.

And she certainly couldn't wear brown leather pants and her usual dress if she wanted to remain under the radar.

Xenia studied Allegra's bare shoulder, her eyes traveling to the yellow, crushed-silk dress. Its high-waisted style had a very Roman feel, but it ended three and a half hand spans above Allegra's knee. It was scandalously short, though mostly appropriate as poolside attire. Partly the reason Allegra had chosen to hide behind the hat and shades.

Her friend completed her examination of Allegra's dress and then sniffed. "Allegra Damascus, you are one woman who couldn't buy fashion sense even if it kicked you in the eye."

"Huh?" Allegra laughed so hard she almost fell off her chair. "What in Apollo's name was that?"

"What?" asked Xenia airily. "Metaphors, dear. I'm sure you know what they are."

"Not sure you're meant to use them like that."

Xenia shook her head and waved her hand at the waiter who came scurrying as if royalty had just summoned him. The look he gave Allegra implied she'd risen in his estimation tenfold just by occupying the same shade as Xenia. Allegra gave him another cheery smile, glad all he could see was her nose, chin, and her bright white teeth.

He took their order of two iced dark Ghanas and sailed between the tables as if Caesar himself had placed the order. Xenia sniffed, glaring at his disappearing back.

"Was he like that to you the entire time?"

Allegra smiled. "I don't mind if it means I can stay out of the limelight. We could be sent home today for all I know. The last thing I need is controversy."

Despite Allegra's words, Xenia didn't seem placated. Her dark skin turned darker as she glared across the patio, and into the room within.

Allegra reached over and grabbed her hand. "Don't make a scene. I want to remain unnoticed."

Xenia laughed at that. "I suppose Pepper and I didn't help much in that regard."

"Not in the least." Allegra squeezed Xenia's hand and asked, "What are you doing in this part of the world anyway?"

Xenia gave another airy shrug. "I was just in the area."

Allegra snorted. "Area?" she asked leaning forward. "I call bullshit," she whispered.

Xenia shook her head. "No good trying to lie—" she stopped sharply, stared down at their hands, where Allegra was still holding onto her fingers, and snatched her hand away. "You...did you..."

Allegra smirked. "Antsy, aren't we?"

Xenia narrowed her eyes and glared at Allegra. "Past experience, you know."

Allegra sighed. "I know. And no. I didn't 'get' anything. It's not consistent. And with the threat that hangs over this place, I don't believe it applies to you. As long as you don't plan on sticking around for too long." The warning in Allegra's voice was all too clear.

And Xenia wasn't oblivious. "Okay, okay. I can take a hint." She scanned the patrons of the restaurant and then said, "What's the special?"

"Charred Pepper Chicken and Crispy Blood Cakes."

Allegra's words hung in the air between the two girls. Xenia's face was suddenly devoid of expression. Allegra hid a smile. She knew very well how Xenia disliked offal of any type.

"Blegh."

Their drinks arrived, saving Allegra from responding as she waited, her eyes on the pool as her drink was set before her and the waiter took their food order.

"Two of your Chicken and Blood. Just make sure mine loses the blood along the way." The waiter grinned widely and wrote the order in his little writing pad. He left, but not before offering Allegra a hesitant smile. She gave him the same cheery grin as before, but it seemed to have the reverse effect to what she'd intended, and he left flustered.

"Guess he doesn't like my smile."

"Not when you smile like a maniacal idiot."

"What?" Allegra knew she should have been insulted, but she was more amused than anything. Xenia had zero ability to get her angry.

Zero.

Xenia leaned forward, her action secretive. She'd be such a bad spy. "So, anyway . . . I have something for you."

Allegra lifted her eyebrows, both curious and wary. Xenia's idea of a surprise bordered on the crazy. She'd once hired a pair of female Sumo oil-wrestlers as a surprise for Allegra all because Allegra had found both Sumo wrestlers and oil wrestlers fascinating.

Xenia was unpredictable.

"So, I'm very well aware you are lacking in the . . . wardrobe department."

"Whatever makes you say that?" Allegra lifted an eyebrow, unable to hide her smile.

Xenia paid her amusement little attention. Instead, she scanned Allegra's dress again and said, "That affront to dress design, for one."

Allegra's jaw dropped. "I'll have you know this was a gift from the ambassador's wife."

Xenia snorted. "Then the ambassador's wife needs to go shopping for fashion sense first before she buys any more clothing, and especially before she thinks she's qualified to dress other people."

"Xenia," Allegra admonished, glancing around her in the hope that her friend's words hadn't been overheard.

Xenia made a rude sound then said, "I've sent some clothing over to your room. I need you to fit them. I think I got the sizing right, but I wanted to be sure."

"Xenia, the last thing I need is to behave like a fashion icon or a Vestal Virgin. You know that's not the way I want to present myself. I may not actually have a choice in much of that image, but I will retain control of the image I want to portray."

"Yeah. An image that has always been one of shriveled up, drugged-up old cronies?"

Allegra didn't dignify that with a response.

"You need to project an image of someone who is beautiful, yet approachable. Mythical, but not untouchable."

"And how do you propose I do that?"

Xenia waved a hand in the air. "By dressing the part. It's where every actor begins."

"I'm not an actor."

"Kid yourself not." Xenia shook her head. "You *are* an actor. You are a figurehead now, whether you want to be or not. Aurelia sequestered herself away from the world because she grew tired of the people's needs, their demands. You can't let that happen to you. You need to project a sense that you are approachable, but only on your terms. Then, and only then, can you dictate where you spend your time."

"I see. And clothing will do that?"

"Clothing." Xenia smiled. "And being a badass."

CHAPTER 7

*A*llegra paced before the wide-open windows. The view from the top of the pyramid was stunning. They'd arrived in the middle of the day, and now, as the sun was beginning to dip beyond the mountains on the horizon, she saw another side of the city.

As the light faded, torches began to flicker around the city, lighting the steps of the multitude of pyramids. Out of the darkness, the stone structures appeared, their rocky surfaces both sinister and beautiful in the flickering golden firelight.

The door to the apartment opened, and Allegra turned on her heel to see Max step into the room. He looked strained and tired, and she suspected the Ambassador hadn't made things easy.

"How did it go?"

Max's lip curled in disgust. "He's being difficult. And I'm yet to figure out why."

"Do you think it's Aulus?"

Max shook his head, but didn't elaborate. Allegra suspected he didn't want to admit that Aulus was more interested in Allegra's success than her failures. She had to wonder though. Aulus had made it very clear he—and the NGS government—wanted the power of the Pythia under their exclusive control.

But, how many things would she really be able to influence on their behalf? Perhaps they wished her to clean up any governmental messes. Or be there to predict if anything was about to go wrong that would affect the interests of the NGS.

Politics was intriguing, but Allegra didn't have the time or the inclination to ponder it.

"You'd think they would want to help us succeed," she murmured as she sank into a nearby armchair.

Max closed in and took the seat across from her. He sighed and leaned into the soft cushions at his back. "To be brutally honest, I have no idea what is going on." He wiped his face and pressed his fingers into his eyes. They were both beginning to feel the effects of jet lag.

"What exactly did he say?" Allegra lifted her bare feet and tucked them under her. She'd soaked in the tub for a while, hoping warmth from the geyser heated water would encourage sleep, but she was oddly rejuvenated after her bath. Not exactly the result she'd wanted.

Max grunted. "Apparently the Qusquan ruling party contacted him while we were still in the air. There was a passenger who'd made a complaint about being mishandled on board—"

"That creep of a man who'd attacked me?"

Max shrugged. "Possibly. He didn't say. What he did impress upon me is that his hands are pretty much tied unless he wants to provoke an international incident."

Allegra's spine stiffened. "Does he realize that blocking my access could also do the same thing?"

"Clearly he is more afraid of angering the Qusquan government than he is of breaking any Treaty of Pythia rules." Max sat forward. "He took me to meet with his contact, but the man gave us the runaround. We sat in their waiting room for an hour only to be told he can't see us."

"What?" Allegra frowned. "That's rude, isn't it. Don't governments follow a more respectful behavioral tradition? I thought the Qusquans still bore a strong Greco-Roman diplomacy ethic."

Max shook his head. "I suspect there is way more going on than just a revocation of a visa."

"You mean a violation of Treaty." Allegra sighed. "Do you think he's being threatened?"

When Max glanced up at her from beneath hooded eyes, Allegra said, "Seems the ambassador didn't want to meet me—which I find strange—so what do you suppose he was afraid of?" Allegra lifted a brow and watched Max straighten.

"You're right. Perhaps he didn't want to have to shake your hand. Had you touched him you may have seen something he'd rather keep to himself."

Max got to his feet and began to pace the patterned carpet. The pile was a deep red, covered in tiny, intricate geometric patterns so distinctive of the Qulla culture.

Max stopped in his tracks and faced Allegra. "That could be it. His behavior was odd, a little bit relaxed and familiar and then a little terse and unhelpful."

"Sounds like something is amiss. We should investigate him further."

Max began to nod, then stopped the movement, his eyes narrowing as he scanned Allegra's face. "Is there a particular reason you're so adamant about him?" Max turned and gave Allegra his undivided attention, his face darkening. "What did you see?"

Allegra gave a delicate shudder. She'd gotten fairly used to the visions over the last few weeks, but she still wasn't entirely comfortable with what she was capable of doing. Max sat on the sofa, the fabric and straw filling giving a low squeak.

The sound brought her attention back to his question. "When

the passenger touched me . . . I saw the destruction as if it was happening at that moment." Allegra paused, barely breathing as she recalled the sight of the city sliding down the side of the mountain. "With the pandemic, it was different, as I saw only what happened after the plague hit."

"But would that be so unusual, considering your first vision was of the city's destruction itself."

Max had a point, and Allegra opened her mouth to agree. But before she replied she realized it wasn't the vision of the city that was bugging her.

Max frowned. "Did you see something else when you touched that man?"

Allegra hid a smile. Since the day he'd walked into her life, attempting to convince her that mythical beings and fairy tales were true, it had felt as if he'd known her all her life.

Max knew her too well. Allegra's smile disappeared at the reminder of their relationship issues. She lifted her chin and kept her features neutral. "What do you know about the ambassador's secretary?"

Max lifted an eyebrow. "Les?

"Is that her name? The dark-haired woman who brought us up?"

Max nodded. "Yes. Les. Celestra Avesta. She's been with the ambassador for two years now."

"So, you know her?" Allegra was beginning to feel like she was pulling teeth. What was Max holding back? She leaned forward. "You know her, don't you?"

He shifted his gaze away. "She used to work for Senator Calvinius in the Capital." Max shifted in his seat then turned his attention back to Allegra, his expression now determined as if he'd made a decision. "I know her because we were together . . . dating . . . for a while."

If Allegra hadn't learned to keep her emotions to herself, she would have flinched from the shock of Max's revelation. Still, Max's face darkened as he studied her lack of response.

Allegra swallowed and uncurled her legs, placing her feet on the ground. "You should have told me."

She hadn't meant it to sound like an accusation, but it did.

Max seemed not to have noticed. He was looking over her shoulder again. "It's just there's baggage there. I didn't want to create more problems. We have enough of our own as it is."

Allegra restrained herself from agreeing. Yes. They had enough of their own problems. But they were in the here and now. For the moment. And she had to tackle the first hurdle, especially coming on the back of Max's relationship revelation.

She cleared her throat. "She touched me."

Max's eyes snapped back to Allegra's face, his eyebrows lifting. "What did you see?" he asked softly.

Allegra pushed to her feet and began to pace the very same line Max had walked only minutes ago.

"She's going to be murdered. I think she may be mixed up in something that could have gotten her killed."

Max got to his feet. "That's a bit vague." His tone was a little sharp, but Allegra took no offense. She'd been deliberately vague. What would he do with the information she could give him?

What could he do?

She sighed and faced him. "I saw her dead. That's all I know. The rest will be supposition and assumption unless you have a way to find out more."

"I will damn well try." Max's voice broke, and he strode away to the window, staring out at the night view. Allegra knew he saw none of its intriguing beauty.

She walked closer to him. "Do you want to tell me a little about her? Maybe if we figure out what she could be involved in, then we could at least try to prevent her death."

Max nodded but still didn't respond.

Allegra shifted to face him, putting a hand on his shoulder. "Is there a way for you to get her recalled to the capital?"

Max startled, glancing at her in surprise. "That's a good idea. She'd have to go and she won't be lying. If she's involved with dangerous people, the fact that the embassy is relocating her would give her a justifiable out that is beyond her control."

"It's a possibility." Max rubbed his chin. "I'll see what I can do. But I think I may need to talk to her first."

"No." Allegra's response was a little too vehement, but she didn't care.

"Allegra." Max spoke patiently as if he was forcing himself to remain calm. "You can't be making decisions for me. Or for Celestra."

Allegra shook her head. She knew what Max was really saying; *You can't tell me what to do when it comes to Celestra.* "Max. I can because *I* was the one who saw her lying there, throat slit, beaten beyond recognition."

Max stiffened. "Beaten beyond recognition?" He paused, color returning to his face. "Maybe it wasn't Les?"

Allegra gripped his arm a little tighter. "I may not have recognized her face, but the dress she is wearing today was on a hanger beside her bed. And I was touching her hand when I got the vision. I don't get visions of people who I am not touching."

Max hung his head. Defeated, he stepped out of her grasp and returned to the sofa. "You're sure it was her?" he asked softly.

"It was her. But if you speak to her about it, you may frighten her. If she still cares for you, she will run if it means protecting you."

"How can you know what she would do?"

"Because it's common sense. And it's what I would do if I were in her position." The moment the words left her mouth, Allegra realized the extent of what he could read into her words.

And when he looked at her she knew he'd read as she'd expected. But they didn't have the time to waste rehashing their own trust issues. More especially since someone else was now playing a key role in their decision-making process.

Max sighed and placed his hands on his hips. "As much as I'd love to keep discussing this, we need to get ready. The ambassador is throwing you a party at his home, and we have two hours to get ready."

"But you need to rest. We both do." What had the ambassador been thinking by making such a sudden arrangement?

"He's doing what he has to do, Allegra. If we are forced to leave here tomorrow how will it look if he hadn't taken advantage of what little time he had while you were here?"

Allegra sighed. "Politics and diplomacy."

"Exactly." They both turned and headed to their rooms. Alone, Allegra contemplated Max's revelation. She'd expected to be furious and jealous. Weren't women supposed to be furious and jealous when their lovers introduced previously-unmentioned girlfriends or wives?

So why was Allegra not jealous?

Was it because she no longer cared for him? Had Max's betrayal on Aulus's instructions really destroyed her affection for him?

She shook her head as she unpacked her suitcase to look for an appropriate dress. Allegra could no more claim to have no feelings for Max than to claim that her blood ran blue instead of red.

The thought of Celestra—though it did not bring on waves of red jealousy—did manage to instill a wave of dislike. Was this perhaps just another form of jealousy? Allegra considered how she felt, but when her stomach began to tighten she pushed the thoughts aside and concentrated on preparing for the evening.

She opened Xenia's box—which she'd run through earlier—and selected a pale peach floor-length dress, laying it on the bed before heading into the bathroom. She'd bathed earlier, so all she had to concentrate on was her makeup.

Xenia was the expert when it came to technique, and Allegra wished for a moment that her friend was there. Not for the makeup; but to give Allegra the moral support she needed.

After touching up her eyes and lips, Allegra sat back and studied her reflection. At times, she didn't recognize the person in the mirror. She was a killer, and it felt a little easier sometimes to pretend the woman reflected back at her was the one responsible for death, the one with blood on her hands.

But then, eventually, Allegra had to give up that fanciful thought and face the truth. *She* was the killer.

A glance down at her hands gave Allegra reason to sigh with relief. For now, they were clean, not a trace of blood in sight.

And Allegra hoped it would stay that way.

CHAPTER 8

*L*ord Severus Langcourt watched the torchlight flicker among the trees in the valley. The blue skies were clear, not a cloud marring its pristine azure beauty. And yet the sight of it pressed down upon him like an unbearable weight, as if he bore Atlas himself upon his head.

He inhaled slowly, attempting to breathe in some calm. Shouldn't the surrounding nature have inspired a little more peace within him? Instead, his stomach clenched hard and he found himself pressing a finger against his jaw and massaging the pain.

It seemed his attempt to escape the stresses of his old life had failed abysmally.

Behind him, his assistant Charles Roquefort was scratching out notes in his book. *I swear the man is obsessed. All he ever does is record everything.*

Roquefort moved closer, coming to stand at the window with Langcourt, who avoided looking at the man's face. It was far too much of a reminder of what had happened to his ancestral home back in Londinium.

Just the memory fueled his rage.

The shouts of warning, the calls from the tunnel watchmen, Langcourt's sudden decision to set the charges. He'd always known that when things came to a head he would never go down without a fight. He'd said he'd rather destroy everything his family had ever built rather than have it taken from them.

And that night he had.

He'd set off the timed bomb, gathered his personal items and had headed to the safe room beneath the villa. He'd built it a long time ago, and it had gone through a number of upgrades. It was bomb proof, disease proof and contained provisions to last ten people for at least five years.

He'd found Roquefort on his way there, injured by an explosion, half his body aflame. Though Langcourt was not particularly selfless, he'd dropped everything to put out the fire and help the man to his feet.

Fortunately, he and Roquefort had made it safely out two days later after the police had left. The crumbled remains of the villa had been scoured and Langcourt had watched them on the various well-positioned cameras around the property.

He'd spent his time watching Roquefort writhe in pain, and had helped tend him to a certain extent. Langcourt didn't possess an iota of nursing skill and had left the man to his own devices, providing him with the necessary first aid, then retreating to the camera to watch what remained of lifetimes of collection.

His anger, his frustration had only grown stronger as he watched them touch his personal possession, and toss his memories into the garbage. When he'd finally left the safe room with Roquefort in tow, he'd walked out of the building without looking back, fearing the sight of it would ruin him.

Something had changed in Roquefort then. He was no longer a sniveling incompetent. His experience had given him a hard streak that sometimes made Langcourt pause. No surprise though, considering the man didn't need a memory to recall the horror of that night. No, all he needed to do was look in the mirror.

Roquefort used to style his hair in a severe, cut-across-the-top-of-the-forehead style. Once it used to remind Langcourt of the ancient senators, of Caesar and his ilk. But no longer.

Now, one-half of Roquefort's face was a mass of crinkled, shiny skin. The left side of his head was almost hairless, the newly healed pink and brown skin sprouting a few short hairs. The burns covered his face, and had ravaged his cheekbones, running all the way down his neck and inside his shirt.

Sometimes Langcourt wished the man would cover his face. He was, after all, not a pretty sight. And he was also a glaring reminder of Langcourt's own failure.

Once, a long time ago, he'd assumed the man didn't have it in him, that he'd never move up the ranks from simpering sycophant. Langcourt was not afraid to admit he was wrong.

Now, Roquefort was his right-hand man, and his skill at translation had helped to no end.

"Sire?"

"Yes, my boy?" Langcourt answered, aware the term was no longer one of superior arrogance, but rather of a bastardized fondness for the burned husk of a man.

"I've made a little more progress on the translations. I've been working out some of it on the computer. Seems they make things a whole lot simpler."

Langcourt didn't respond. This was classified as small talk, and he didn't have time to waste on chitchat.

"I think we will have something concrete to go on within the week." The man hesitated which made Langcourt impatient.

"What is it, man? Stop waffling and spit it out."

"We have word from the capital."

"And?"

"The Pythia Allegra landed in Qusqu late this morning."

Langcourt found his ears were ringing so loudly he had to ask Roquefort to repeat his next sentence.

"The government officials have placed some sort of hold on her visa. They'd granted her temporary stay overnight until they resolve the problem."

He'd come all the way across the world only for the bitch to follow him there. Last time Allegra Damascus had been instrumental in his destruction, and he wasn't planning on letting her win. Not this time.

"How long will she be here?"

"With some luck, only overnight."

"What's the problem with the visa?"

"Bureaucratic red tape, sire. My source tells me there is a suspicion of collusion with the NGS."

Langcourt clicked his tongue and waved an irritated hand in the air. "I couldn't care less what the problem is. What I need to know is how long she will be here, and if and when do you arrange access?"

"Access?" Roquefort shifted from one foot to the other, his eyes flitting from his book to Langcourt and back. "Why do we need access to her?"

Langcourt grunted and moved away from the brightness at the window. His mood did not suit sunshine and warmth. He glared at Roquefort. "Have you looked in the mirror lately? Can you not see what she's done to you?"

Roquefort's eyes went hard, and he lifted a hand to his mottled cheek. "She didn't…"

"Maybe not with her own hand, but she sent them our way."

"I can see how she can be tangentially responsible. But what do you have in mind?" The man had changed. A month ago, he'd have agreed the Pythia was to blame and set his mind instantly to a plan for vengeance.

Langcourt wasn't sure if the man's newly formed spine was a good thing or not.

"I want to obtain direct access to her."

"To kill her?"

"As much as I would like for that to be my instant response, I do believe we need to be smarter about her this time. We underestimated her last time."

"She had help."

"Yes. It's the nature of that help that worries me."

"Yes, sire. Her escape was nothing short of miraculous. On the divine intervention level, to be honest."

Langcourt stiffened. As much as his assistant sometimes rambled nonsensically, he had moments in which brilliance spewed forth. This was one of those moments.

"Divine intervention, did you say?" His assistant nodded. "I do believe you have just hit the nail on the head, my boy."

Langcourt hid a satisfied grin. He may yet obtain the revenge he longed for. The Pythias were responsible for so much destruction, most especially to his own bloodline. They'd taken so much from his family over the centuries, but the most recent blow was by far the hardest to endure.

All his family's history had been within the walls of his ancestral villa. Everything within the building had been razed to the ground. Relics and spoils of war from across the world had occupied the house, every corner, every table set with history.

Now all gone.

The Langcourt family history was now erased from record. And Langcourt had had to run, to go into hiding, afraid for his life because everywhere he turned someone was looking for him. Everywhere he turned someone was waiting to betray him.

Langcourt inhaled sharply and began to pace. "Where is your investigation into the Pythia's lineage?"

"I'm afraid, sire, that once we . . . left home, the investigation came to a halt. The translations here in the ruins, have taken priority. Do you wish me to focus on the Pythia for now?"

They had arrived, both he and Roquefort in the employ of the high priest, tasked with translating the writings of a long dead shaman. Langcourt had, in his own time, been adept at translations and had considered the job as a means to an escape.

As distasteful as it was, he knew he had to do something in order to make money. He had half a dozen bank accounts around the world holding all sorts of riches from rare gems to gold bullion, but he wasn't about to approach any one of them yet. Not until the search for him had died down.

He could wait. And in the meantime he could enjoy the translations.

He was close to finishing up, and Roquefort had proved adept at transcribing the work he did. The High Priest expected an answer within days, and Langcourt knew he'd deliver on time.

Given his current progress he believed he could do without his assistant's constant attendance.

"I do believe Allegra Damascus must now be our priority, my dear boy." Langcourt nodded firmly at his decision. "Keep me informed. I want updates four times a day. More if there are significant developments. Use the agents in Fornia for the groundwork there."

Excitement flashed in Roquefort's eyes, and Langcourt wasn't surprised; genealogy was the man's forte after all.

A giant shadow blocked out the sun as Langcourt strode to the window, searching the vista. He spotted the creature toward the left of the pyramid he occupied, flying overhead now in a shallow arc.

A giant golden condor.

The birds were majestic, their wingspan rivaling even the albatross from the Brittanic Isles.

The sight of the powerful bird revived Langcourt's confidence.

Power and might such as he had were something one could not take down with a single swipe. He was stronger than they knew.

He just had to strike smart. And strike hard. And then he would move in for the death blow.

A death blow to the Pythia.

CHAPTER 9

The residential suburbs of Qusqu were set back from the city, somewhat protected by forested land giving the area an air of untouched beauty.

The homes here in Peru were oddly similar to those in the States, the latest architecture vied for space with buildings reminiscent of ancient mud-wall buildings. Still, the combination seemed to work well enough that the street provided a beautiful view.

The darkness hindered much of their visibility, though torches lit not only the buildings but the street-corners too. The city had seen fit to provide the residents with street-lighting, not unusual in this day and age, but not common enough to be taken for granted.

The ambassador's gated property was guarded by two fierce-looking sentries. They both wore the standard blood-red skirts and gold body armor, but that was as far as it went in terms of a fashionable statement of class.

Allegra was relieved to see the ambassador hadn't participated in the latest trend where house staff were dressed and treated like the lowliest of slaves. The new trend, a mere reflection of ancient times, had elicited a lot of negative publicity with people complaining it encouraged exploitation of staff.

Allegra could understand completely having seen it first-hand not too long ago in the home of a well-known tennis player. The memory reminded her she'd only had her visions for a short time, which explained why she was struggling with them. It wasn't as if she could pick up the phone and ask another oracle for advice.

McIvor had sent a car for them, and now, as they drew up in front of the house, Allegra glanced at Max. He'd been quiet the entire drive which was pretty unusual for him. He was always the one trying to put her at ease.

The car slowed and then jerked to a stop as the two sentries began to open the giant wrought-iron gates.

The short drive up to the entrance was lined with over-hanging wide-leaved emerald-green fronds of trees and plants Allegra was unfamiliar with. Fauna and flora were not her forte.

Still, despite her lack of interest in species and subspecies of plants, Allegra was able to appreciate the beauty of the gardens and the lost-in-the-jungle atmosphere it evoked.

When they drew up in front of the house, Max grunted. Allegra was already frowning as she turned to glance at him, not surprised to find him studying the mansion with much the same expression as she had.

"Ostentatious?" she said beneath her breath.

"Very."

"Unusual?"

"Very."

"There is a residence within the embassy building, isn't there?" Allegra asked.

Max nodded. "A floor below the offices, and one above where we are staying."

"So . . . is McIvor independently wealthy?"

"Not that I know of. Neither him nor his wife came from this type of money." Max pursed his lips. "I find it curious. On a government salary, this type of grandeur is suspicious."

"Makes it all suspicious. Do you think he's on the take?"

Max shrugged. "I can't guess until I know more. We've got our work cut out for us. If he's deep enough in their pockets, then there is a chance you and I will be on the next plane out."

"Guess we need to be on our best behavior then."

"That's what I was afraid of," said Max as he opened the door and helped Allegra out.

The long skirt of Xenia's creation slid to the ground, and Allegra felt almost regal. Her friend certainly possessed the taste Allegra lacked. It was a pity Xenia couldn't have been with them tonight, but Allegra had insisted she leave as soon as possible. There was no way she was about to risk her friend's life, especially not in the face of actually knowing something was about to go terribly wrong. She'd seen Xenia die once before. And even though it had been a prophesied death that had eventually been averted, Allegra did not want to have to see such a thing again.

Now she walked up the steps to the entrance of the ambassador's home, one which could be called palatial by any standards. The Roman architecture with its tall columns and stone frontages should have seemed out of place within the city, but with the residences along the street, all so different from each other, the mansion was no more unusual than the pyramid next door and the minarets across the street.

A line of people waited at the entrance, all entering at the announcement of their names. Allegra's heart thudded in her throat. She hated being put on show and she knew this was exactly what it appeared to be; the Pythia being paraded around for all to see. And as quickly as possible in case she was required to leave the country the next day.

"Allegra Damascus. The Lady Pythia, Oracle of the Ages. Escorted by Commander Maximus Vissarion of the New Germanic States."

Max gave her his arm, and she latched onto it, while keeping her fingers out of her range of sight. At the moment, they were nice and clean, but it was safer to not look at all. Perhaps the dramatic entrance was distracting her, but she couldn't assume she wouldn't experience an attack tonight.

That would be presumptuous.

They descended a set of six stairs, lined on either side by trees and fronds, interspersed with golden statues and gigantic amphorae. The ambassador and his wife—a small gilt-haired woman—were waiting for them at the bottom of the stairs, and McIvor turned toward them, his glance sweeping and somewhat surprised, as if he'd only just realized they'd arrived.

Given the announcement had likely deafened every person present, Allegra thought the fakery was stupid on the part of the ambassador. All he'd managed to do was lower himself in her esteem by a few more points.

He held out his hand to indicate their arrival, and Max and Allegra went to the couple.

"My Lady. Welcome to our humble abode."

Oh dear.

"May I introduce you to my wife, Elana." Elana McIvor held out her hand, clearly unconscious or ignorant of what could be in store for her.

Before Allegra could do anything in response, Max reached for the woman's hand and pumped it cheerfully. "Thank you so much for opening your beautiful home to use, Elana."

Elana blushed. "It was only my pleasure. We are honored to have the Pythia within our home." She met Allegra's gaze. "Please . . . my home is your home . . . and I mean that sincerely. I only wish you could have stayed with us—"

"Dear, I don't think we should concern ourselves with politics tonight." He gave her a glance that was filled with some unsaid message. One Elana received and felt admonished enough to blush deeply again.

Allegra's eyes narrowed as she watched McIvor, and she decided she was no longer going to tolerate his boorish behavior. She took a step closer to his wife. "Elana. You must tell me. Is that your natural hair color?"

Elana beamed as she touched her copper hair. "Yes, it is. Isn't it wonderful?"

Allegra would have been taken aback by such self-praise, but oddly enough it seemed Elana was totally devoid of vanity. She spoke of her stunning hair as she would have of a beautiful sunrise. Not something to own, but rather something that just was.

"It certainly is wonderful." Allegra stepped away, glancing over at the table filled with canapés and Elana took the hint. She was, after all, a diplomat's wife.

"I hope you forgive me, but I won't introduce you around. Not everyone here would expect to meet the Pythia face-to-face, and if we walked over and introduced you, we may frighten some of them."

"Oh dear." Allegra's stomach twinged.

"Oh, no. Please take no offense. It's just access to the Oracle is seen as an exclusive thing within the Qusquan tradition. And there's a hierarchy we really shouldn't breach."

Allegra respected that and deferred to Elana's diplomatic understanding. Over the next half hour, Elana pointed out at least three dozen influential business-owners, officials and high-ranking members of the Qusquan government.

Elana never faded, keeping up the small talk, feeding Allegra with both bites of food and local gossip. The woman was completely guileless, and Allegra was left to wonder how she'd ended up married to the pretentious and manipulative McIvor.

Just when Allegra was beginning to feel a headache coming, Elana waved down a tall man, whose clean-shaven face and angular bone structure marked him as of Aztec in ancestry. He walked over, his gait smooth and unhurried and gave Allegra a polite smile.

"General Qhapaq, have you met Lady Allegra?" Elana waved at Allegra.

The general bowed briefly and then straightened. "I have not yet had the pleasure."

With jet lag still running thickly through Allegra's veins, she moved forward automatically, her hand outstretched to shake the General's. But she found her hand hovering in the air, with the general glaring at it as if it were a spitting viper.

CHAPTER 10

"My Lady, you may forgive me if I do not touch you." The general's eyes flashed coldly as he spoke.

Allegra stiffened, then smiled. "I apologize, General Qhapaq. I'm just a little tired after the long trip. I forgot for a moment."

The general bowed, but from his expression, it was clear he didn't believe her. He walked off, mumbling some excuse about having to speak to someone, leaving Elana staring at Allegra, her mouth open.

"Now what in the world was that about?" she said, her eyes following the general who crossed the room and whispered something to an aide, then glanced over at the two women. His eyes were filled with suspicion.

Allegra sighed. "I'm sorry, Elana. It's clear you are not aware . . . but sometimes all it takes to see a person's future is a simple touch. Some people know about the intricacies of how the seeing works, and it seems the general believes we are here to dupe him in some way. To extract his future from him on the pretense of a handshake."

"Oh dear," Elana breathed the shocked words. She took a step forward. "Perhaps we need to explain to him. I'm afraid that would put a strain on diplomatic relations, and if Liam were to find out, he'd be upset."

Allegra touched Elana's shoulder, ensuring her fingers met only fabric. "You'll be wasting your time. What's done is done, and should you try to fix it, it will likely make things worse." Allegra bent her head to meet the woman's eyes. "Just let it alone. We will explain what happened. If it comes to that."

Somewhat comforted, Elana led Allegra around the room to meet up with her husband again. As they approached Allegra caught sight of a dark-haired woman bending close to Max's ear.

Celestra.

Allegra found a sudden heat fill her gut, the energy pushing her to move faster, as if to get to Max's side before . . . before what? Allegra shook her head. What was wrong with her? Was it possible she *was* jealous?

Allegra shook her head. She was not the jealous type.

As she reached Max's side, Celestra looked up and met Allegra's eyes. A smile formed on her lips, friendly, unconscious, until she straightened and looked over Allegra's shoulder. Then the smile disappeared, and her lips formed a thin line.

Allegra glanced over her shoulder, but the only person she saw in Celestra's line of sight was the general.

Odd.

Allegra gave Max a stiff glare and moved toward Celestra. Max took the hint and moved to talk to McIvor and his wife while Allegra shifted to Celestra's side, giving her a smile as she leaned over the table to grab a piece of orange corncake. "I'm not sure what's going on with you . . . but I feel I must tell you that I touched you."

That was all she needed to say.

Celestra stiffened then gave Allegra a surreptitious glance. She too reached for a piece of the cake, and as she turned away to rest the knife back onto the knife-plate, she said, "I'll come to your room tonight."

Then she turned, glared at Allegra coldly and walked off.

Allegra went cold. Whatever Celestra was up to, her acting ability had been developed beyond the talent of even some of the highest-paid award-winning actors on the silver screen to date.

Considering she lived her life at the business end of a deadly blade—taking into account the way her life is meant to end—Allegra was not surprised.

The rising volume of the orchestra at the other end of the room drew Allegra's attention.

McIvor moved toward his wife who smiled as he took her hand and led her to the dance floor, which quickly emptied of the guests. A crowd had gathered along the four sides of the floor, and a rush of applause filled the room.

Max moved closer to Allegra's side, his expression when he glanced at her confirming he hadn't expected the display.

The music rose, dramatic notes that fell to almost silence before it picked up again. As if hearing a cue—which Allegra was unable to identify—the ambassadorial couple began to dance. Elana's dress shimmered in the light as her husband gripped her waist and spun with her in a wide circle. His gaze, though on his wife's face seemed to flit around the room as if in search of someone.

Celestra came to stand at Allegra's side, then leaned forward to look pointedly at Max. "I believe it's your turn."

"I don't dance."

She gave her a sly smile. "Of course, you do." Then she paused and met Allegra's eyes. "Sometimes you don't have much of a choice in these things. You should dance if you hope to not offend the ambassador's graciousness. And the Pythia would not want to be seen as rude." The woman's voice seemed to soften, and then her expression hardened, as if she'd suddenly remembered something. Then her eyes shuttered, and she stepped away from Allegra and Max.

"We should listen to her," Allegra murmured to Max, her eyes on the couple swaying to the music.

"Fine. Had I known I would have made an effort to practice." He gave her his elbow. "Just don't be surprised when I tread on your toes."

Allegra gave him a humorless smile and curved her hand around his elbow, allowing him to lead her to the dance floor. As they moved, she kept an eye on the guests, taking in faces, expressions, body language. Whoever was influencing McIvor was good at not showing their hand tonight. Not even once.

Unless General Qhapaq was involved.

Allegra filed that thought away and concentrated on not dancing on Max's toes. He'd lied about his inability to dance, and she glanced up at his face, narrowing her eyes at him.

"You can dance." Her tone was accusatory.

He shrugged as he took her hand to send her into a double twirl. Bringing her close to his chest he said, "I don't like being on display."

"Then you'd better get used to it considering you are always on display when you are at my side . . . And I am always on display."

His expression darkened and then Max snorted. "When people see you, I don't think they even know I am there. You are the one they come to see."

Allegra didn't want to get into an argument with him about what she stood for, as opposed to what she wanted to stand for.

They danced for a few minutes, and Allegra allowed herself to enjoy the feel of his body against hers. They hadn't spoken much in the last few days, the hurt in her heart making it difficult to converse with him without remembering his betrayal. She'd been afraid of breaking down if they broached the subject, but she knew the time would come when she had to accept the change in their relationship.

Max had continued as if nothing had happened, and at some level that hurt more than anything. Part of her had wanted him to challenge her, to demand she listen to his side of the story, but instead he'd stepped back and said nothing, preferring to skirt the issue entirely.

Max's palm pressed against her spine a little too hard. A warning. She forced a bright smile to her face and lifted her gaze to meet his. He seemed unable to convey the message and merely held himself stiff.

At her side, Allegra noticed General Qhapaq request a dance with Elana leaving the ambassador partnerless in the middle of his own dance floor. Another hint of pressure at her back and Max slowed the dance, drawing to a stop beside McIvor, who appeared a little off balance at being stranded at his own party.

When Allegra leaned to him, he smiled with relief, reaching for her arm. Allegra wasn't sure if he'd intended to touch her, or if he'd remembered he shouldn't. It was possible he was merely so flustered he'd forgotten who she was.

Or what she could see.

She took his outstretched arm, placing her fingers on his shoulder, very aware of his movements as he curled his left arm around her waist. She tried to relax, knowing what Max wanted her to do.

What better way to get a little more information on the ambassador than to see his future. A vision may hold the key to details of what was to come.

McIvor lifted his other hand, and Allegra took it, allowing her bare palm to touch his.

Her vision shifted, and she struggled to breathe as the room fell away. A cry left her lips, but she wasn't sure if she'd uttered the sound aloud or if it was just in her head.

McIvor sat on the floor, not two feet from Allegra, his eyes wide open, blood smearing his cheeks and forehead. That he was dead was painfully obvious from the sight of two things. The spear that emerged from his skull, an inch above his left eye.

And the fact that his head was no longer attached to his body.

CHAPTER 11

The vision filled Allegra's senses, and she swallowed slowly, trying hard to remain calm, to not reveal to their entire audience that she'd just had a vision.

She forced the muscles in her fingers to remain relaxed as they held onto McIvor's shoulder, forced her lips to smile, forced her legs to continue dancing, to not flinch every time she came into contact with his skin.

She swallowed the urge to laugh; it could have been worse—she could have passed out.

This very room, where she now danced with the ambassador, was the same room in which he would die with an ancient ritual spear through his skull.

But, she'd won out against her emotions, against the scene of horror still overlaying her vision.

In the end, Allegra kept her cool and completed the dance. She felt McIvor's warm, clammy palms against her hand as he led her to the edge of the dance floor to a round of applause.

He made a show of leading Allegra to Max and Elana who were both standing beside the table where they'd abandoned their food.

McIvor handed her over to Max with a flourish that made Allegra feel slightly ill. The man had an oily layer beneath his very polished exterior.

Elana was smiling, her expression disarming, but Allegra was aware of her now, and most thankful her radar had strengthened regarding the woman.

Though she smiled there was a tightness at the corners of her eyes, an odd way she held her head, making Allegra more certain than ever that something was off.

"My Lady, you are a wonderful dancer," Elana spoke in a gushing tone and made Allegra want to shudder.

Instead, she smiled and said, "Well, I'm not so sure about that, Elana. I do believe it was your husband who kept me on my toes. You're very lucky he doesn't step on your toes."

Elana laughed in response, appearing a little more relaxed now, which led Allegra to wonder if perhaps the woman was merely the jealous type.

As the laughter died down, Allegra sensed someone at her back. Celestra—who'd been standing at Max's side and was handing Allegra a glass of wine—stiffened, her eyes on something over Allegra's shoulder.

Allegra turned and was startled as she came face to face with General Qhapaq. She glanced up at him, a ripple of unease skimming her nape at his expression—displeasure bordering on anger.

"My Lady," he said tipping his head forward. "You dance well."

Allegra smiled and reached for the glass Celestra had forgotten to pass. She lifted the glass to the General in a mock toast. "Thank you, General. It's kind of you to say so."

There was a moment of silence that was filled with the simmering drumbeat and slowly rising tempo of violins as the orchestra began a new set. The general remained silent, stretching out the tension. She knew that technique. Tox, her ex-boyfriend, had employed it one too many times.

"I am curious, my Lady. It is my understanding that you would receive a vision using touch." Allegra could have sworn she felt the tension around her rise.

"Yes, General. I believe that is the reason you didn't shake my hand earlier." Allegra was shocked that the words had popped out of her mouth before she could stop them. Still, she was at the point in the evening where she cared far too little. More than anything it was the admonition in the general's tone that had gotten under her skin.

General Qhapaq looked over her shoulder at McIvor, and asked Allegra, "My Lady, am I to assume then that you have received a vision of our ambassador's future?"

Allegra narrowed her eyes. Who did he think he was to ask such a question. And why was he so inquisitive at all? What does he hope to gain from a vision of McIvor's future?

Allegra let out a soft laugh—hoping it sounded flirty. Weren't men distracted by that? She studied the general's eyes. "I'm afraid it doesn't work that way. Not entirely. So, unfortunately, I have to disappoint you. I had no vision of the ambassador's future." Allegra paused and lifted her chin. "And even if I had, I would certainly not be at liberty to reveal the contents of such a vision to you without the express permission of Ambassador McIvor himself."

The general appeared unconcerned with his rudeness, nor did he appear bothered by Allegra's rebuke. "I'm sure our ambassador would not mind." He gave a small bow again. "In any event, it appears it matters not at all. If you didn't see his future." Again, the general seemed to be pushing for an answer.

Allegra shook her head. "Unfortunately, my visions are unpredictable. Sometimes I don't see anything." She glanced at McIvor over her shoulder and smiled. "Perhaps Ambassador McIvor has nothing in his future that he should be concerned about. Except of course his wife if he doesn't complete their dance." Allegra hoped the smile on her face was a teasing one.

The couple laughed, and McIvor was already leading his wife off when Allegra turned to face the general again. The man seemed unaffected in such a way that Allegra wanted to wave her hand in front of his eyes and ask if anyone was home. She'd heard of people who suffered from a muscular degenerative disease of the face which prevented them from smiling, or even laughing. Perhaps the forbidding general was one of them.

She almost opened her mouth to speak when the general straightened and gave her that small half-nod that constituted a bow. "I must take your leave, my Lady. I confess I am disappointed. I had hoped to hear something interesting about Ambassador McIvor, but perhaps it is as you say and he is safe."

Something trilled within Allegra as she made a mental record of the man's word choices. She'd barely given him a smile before he was turning and stalking off across the room, weaving between the dancing couples and heading to a small group of government officials.

The dance was over within minutes, and Elana returned, pulling her husband by his sleeve. "Come darling. You must send the Lady Pythia home before she falls asleep on her feet. Jet lag can be an awful thing if one doesn't get sufficient rest."

McIvor nodded. "I'll get them to bring the car around."

As he walked over to Max and Celestra, Elana asked Allegra, "Are you sure you didn't see anything?"

Allegra shook her head. "Sorry. Nothing."

"My Lady, I hope you don't think you need to protect us from any vision you may see. We can handle anything you may need to tell us."

Allegra forced herself to chuckle. "I assure you, Elana, I would tell you if I'd seen anything. But, as much as I'd like to say yes, that would be a lie."

Elana's eyes hardened, and Allegra got the feeling again that the woman knew more than she let on. Probably would be a good idea to get Max to keep an eye on Elana as well. She was certainly not as innocent as she'd let on.

Allegra leaned closer, a conspiratorial hush to her tone. "Elana, if you do want some private time with me, I'm happy to try to access my visions for you, or for your husband." Elana blinked, taken aback by the direct offer.

She'd seemed so eager to know, and Allegra would have thought she'd agree instantly. But Elana hesitated as if the thought of having her future foretold was distasteful.

So, if the McIvors weren't the type to want their future told, then why was Elana so keen to know what Allegra had seen?

Or was it that she was afraid of what Allegra *could* have seen?

The actions of someone who had something to hide.

So, what were the McIvors into? Allegra suppressed a sigh.

"Thank you for the offer, my Lady. I will let Liam know. See what he says." She spoke brightly, a forced enthusiasm filling her tone.

Allegra nodded. "I'm at your service," she said softly as Elana beckoned her to follow to McIvor, who now stood near the doorway with Max at his side. Celestra was nowhere to be seen.

Allegra turned to give Elana one last smile, and her eyes were drawn beyond the woman's shoulder. Through her lashes, she looked across the room to see the general watching her.

Beside him stood a tall, gaunt man, his dark eyes hooded, cheekbones sunken. He too was staring at Allegra, his expression like granite.

Allegra pretended ignorance

The attention of both men certainly raised suspicions, but the memories of what she'd seen still swam across her vision.

They said their goodbyes and headed to the waiting car, Max's hand on her back giving her another warning pressure. He handed her into the back seat and slid in beside her.

"Don't worry. It shouldn't take too long to get back. I'm sorry it took so long."

Allegra gave a sigh, aware now that Max meant she shouldn't say anything while in the car. The engine was loud, but not enough to mask all of their conversation.

It didn't matter anyway. Allegra was far too exhausted to say a word.

All she wanted was to wipe away the horror from her memory.

And yet, all she saw was the bloody tip of a deadly spear. And McIvor's head rolling on the floor beside his body.

CHAPTER 12

*T*he drive back had taken longer than Allegra had expected. Most probably because she was exhausted, both by the jet lag and the vision. It had been a while since a vision had knocked her back so hard.

By the time they walked into their apartment, her hands were shaking, and she was shivering.

Max frowned, curling his arm around her shoulders and rubbing her hands. "You're frozen," he murmured guiding her to the room. "Should I run a bath, or would a shower be okay?"

Allegra shook her head, then nodded, then laughed softly. "A shower will do just fine. I need to get warm, not drown in the tub."

"I won't let you drown. I'll be right here," he said, giving her a wink.

"You most certainly will not." The last thing Allegra needed was Max and his all-too-attractive self invading her personal space when she'd passed the point of exhaustion.

"Fine." Max pouted in mock disappointment. "But I will be waiting outside just in case. And don't lock the door."

"Why ever not?"

"Because if you pass out in the shower, I don't want to have to break the door down to get inside." There was a sneaky smile on his face, but Allegra knew she could trust him.

Still, she couldn't help but flush a little at the thought of him being so nearby while she showered.

More out of concern that Max would come looking for her if she spent too long in the shower and actually passing out, Allegra spent only a few minutes under the hot spray. When she stepped out and toweled dry, she was warmed up enough that she no longer shivered.

Wrapped within the thick towel, Allegra headed for the door, aware she hadn't even thought about bringing her night clothes in to change. It didn't matter though. Hadn't Max seen her almost naked a couple times already?

So why was the prospect so unnerving all of a sudden?

As Allegra stepped out of the bathroom, Max called her over to the small sitting area and handed her a mug. Steam rose from the dark surface, and Allegra smiled.

Chocolate.

One of her favorites, as Max well knew. Still in her towel, Allegra curled up on the sofa and sipped the drink, blowing lightly on the surface as she drank.

The groan she let out had Max laughing out loud.

"What?" she asked with a smile.

"It's not safe to make sounds like that especially while wearing next to nothing."

Allegra laughed. "Seems like you haven't tasted this chocolate before. It's like drinking liquid heaven."

Max was nodding. "I've heard it described as orgasmic."

Allegra nodded, her expression serious. "I do believe that is the best word. I'd always loved the drink, but they must be doing something different here because it's simply divine."

Max smiled, seeming to enjoy her delight in the drink. Before she'd come to Qusqu, she'd thought the chocolate drink simply delicious, and had indulged as often as she could.

Now she had to admit she'd never tasted the real thing before.

She sighed and sat back, more than a little disappointed that her mug was empty.

"So . . . what did you see?"

"Was it that obvious?"

"Only to me."

She sighed. "That's good. I thought I'd lied pretty well."

"You did. You almost had me convinced."

Allegra squeezed her eyes shut and felt a wave of fatigue wash over her. "He was on the floor. There was so much blood you couldn't see the white tiles any longer. Someone killed him—a spear to the skull. They hit him from behind, so there is a chance he never knew it was coming." Allegra paused, taking a breath because she felt like she was rolling down the side of a mountain being chased by an avalanche. "His head . . . he'd been decapi- tated. But the spear was still in his head. At least when I saw him."

Max nodded, his expression telling Allegra nothing of what he thought. "Any other details? Anyone else in the vision?"

Allegra paused. "I think I may have seen Elana in the back- ground, but I couldn't see how badly she was hurt or if she was even alive."

"Was there anything that made you believe she was hurt."

She shook her head. "No. I just caught a flash in the background. I could be wrong too. Maybe it wasn't her, but I feel like it was her."

"Then we will trust your senses. Your visions may bring you more than just sight."

"So, what do you think it meant? Do you think I really did see him die?"

Max shrugged. "Considering your track record, I'd say yes." He offered a rueful smile.

Allegra blinked, and a flash of the vision hit her. McIvor's eyes wide open and lifeless. The spear emerging from just above his left eye, the skull punctured and bloody. The iron spear, its sharp triangular point glistening with blood and brain matter.

"There was a spear. I think it may have been something ancient. Aztec maybe."

"You're thinking his murder could be ritualistic?"

"It's certainly possible given where we are. Many of the tribes in the area go back centuries and still practice their own traditions."

Allegra sighed again. "Whatever the case is, there is one thing we can be sure of. If McIvor is somehow involved and is in danger from the people controlling him, it means he's dispensable."

"And it means the people pulling his puppet strings are very powerful."

"Do you think his involvement could be connected to Celestra's death in the vision?"

Allegra contemplated it. "It could be. The violence is certainly a common factor."

"Maybe Celestra can tell us more," said Max. "I'll see if I can convince her to talk to us."

"You won't need to."

Max raised an eyebrow.

"I had a word with her at the ball. She said she'd drop by as soon as she could."

Max's lips formed a thin line.

Allegra got to her feet. "I'd better put some clothes on." Allegra hurried to her room and paused on the threshold. "Oh, there was one other thing. I think we need to keep an eye on Elana. There was just something about her that felt off. As if she was hiding something."

Max nodded. "I agree. Seems you and I are on the same wavelength."

"And I think we need to keep a spotlight on General Qhapaq."

"I could not agree more."

"The man gave me the chills."

"He was damned disrespectful is what he was."

"Max, not everyone cares about the Pythia. He's clearly someone important within his tribe, and for all we know, he's a priest of a tribal religion. Their beliefs clash wildly with ours. We can't force our traditions on them."

Max shook his head and got to his feet, walking over to the window. "That's the last thing I'd want to do. It's just that nobody ever disrespected Aurelia that way. I don't see why they should do that to you."

She shrugged. "I'm young, inexperienced. Ignorant too. Why should they put their belief in me? Just because I can see the future?" She shook her head. "I don't think people are that easily controlled. They need to see proof that I have their best interests at heart. And I just have to keep going as I've been. Doing the right thing to show everyone what I'm about. Aurelia had decades to prove herself. I was literally born yesterday."

CHAPTER 13

*M*ax stared at Allegra's face, and she watched him watch her. There was so much more she wanted to say but fatigue and a sense of propriety forced her to retreat within the room and slip into her nightgown.

Courtesy of Xenia, the plum silk, and lace concoction was more suitable for a honeymoon than a diplomatic trip. Thankfully it came with a more sedate wrap, and minutes later Allegra left the room to find Max ushering Celestra inside.

The woman's eyes appeared haunted, as if they struggled to hold within them secrets she knew would cause untold damage.

Or perhaps it was only Allegra's precognition that allowed her the luxury to speculate.

Celestra held on tightly to her purse as Allegra walked toward her. "You came," Allegra said softly, waving a hand to the small seating arrangement near the window.

Celestra's smile was tight as she took a prim seat on the edge of the sofa. "Not exactly."

Allegra's stomach tightened. If Celestra evaded their questions, it would mean they'd need to start investigating from a different angle. Allegra forced herself to remain calm, and she took a seat and waited as Max offered the secretary a drink—which she refused.

She studied the interaction between the two of them, wondering at the unspoken familiarity between them. The way Max prepared the coffee even though Celestra had refused, how he knew how much cream she took, or the way he handed it over to her, handle turned toward her. So much care in his actions.

Again, Allegra's gut twinged, but this time she knew that emotion; one she wasn't proud of.

Jealousy.

When Max took a seat beside Allegra, Celestra set her mug back on the coffee table between them. "I came to give you these." She opened the flap of her large purse and withdrew a brown envelope. Handing it to Max, she said, "Your visas have been approved, and your passports stamped and returned. There is a formal apology included in the envelope. Two in fact. One from the Qusquan president and the other from the ambassador."

Allegra forced herself to hide a smirk. That McIvor was coming to the party now was far too convenient. Something had changed tonight, and Allegra would have bet her entire meager inheritance it had had something to do with her lack of prophetic vision when she'd touched McIvor.

Had she lulled them into a false sense of security? Did they think they were safe, believing she'd seen nothing? Was that why General Qhapaq was so interested?

And now, were they about to risk it all by asking Celestra for information that could endanger them?

She forced herself to concentrate when Celestra spoke. "Please let us know if there is anything you need. The apartment is yours, and we will have a vehicle allocated to you for your personal use. I've arranged for a security detail as well . . . all NGS military, Max. So, you won't need to worry."

Max smiled, and Allegra found her lips turning up too. They were already worried about high-ranking officials of the NGS like the ambassador and his secretary, what made them think a mere army officer would be immune to influence.

Celestra surprised them by moving to stand. "I should be going. I've kept you too long. You both need some sleep after all this drama."

Allegra shook her head, though she didn't move. "How is McIvor involved?"

"Involved in what?"

Allegra maintained eye contact with Celestra, watching to see if the woman was about to lie. "Something is very wrong here. I'm just not sure where the problem is. It could be McIvor involved with a few unsavories and if so we'd need to know. Before the president sends in his investigative team. They'll tear the whole embassy apart."

Celestra's mouth dropped open, and she shifted her gaze to Max, her expression pleading.

But Max shook his head. "She's right, Les. They'd bring the maximum weight down on him if they think he's involved in something."

The woman shook her head and sat back down while Allegra leaned forward watching her closely. "Celestra?" Only when the woman looked up and met her gaze did Allegra continue. "Who's threatening you?"

Celestra's skin was pale to begin with, but her milky complexion shifted to a sickly gray at Allegra's words.

Allegra refused to let up. "What do they have on you?"

Celestra shook her head. "I don't know what you are trying to get at. Nobody is threatening me. No one has anything on me. I'm not even sure what you mean by that."

Allegra's jaw hardened. She got to her feet and began to pace. "They are going to kill you."

The woman fell silent as she stared at Allegra's face. Then she smiled. "I know what you're trying to do. You want to trap me. This is a trap, right?" She looked at Max again, her eyes pleading. She probably wanted it all to be a joke, or a mistake.

"How are you involved, Celestra?" asked Allegra as she strode over and sat beside the woman. She registered the incongruity for a moment, her sexy nightwear did nothing to herd her intimidation tactics. Allegra lowered her voice. "What do they have on you? It's in your own best interest to come clean."

Celestra shook her head, leaning away from Allegra.

Allegra could see it in her eyes, that deer-in-the-headlights look that told Allegra the poor woman was so in over her head she probably had no idea how to get herself out.

She'd been debating whether or not to play hardball, but Celestra's reluctance only served to make Allegra more determined.

"They are going to kill you."

Max glanced over at Allegra, his expression shocked. Probably not as shocked as Allegra herself was at the word.

But Celestra let out a sad laugh, and her shoulders slumped. "I suppose it doesn't make a difference anyway. I'm too close to you. They'll never believe it if I said I didn't speak with you about it."

"So, is someone forcing you to do something you don't want to?" Max asked softly.

"Of course not. The revolution deserved a chance, and I'll do anything I can to serve the progress of the revolution. Even give my life." Allegra frowned. Celestra's words had sounded way too rote, as if she'd memorized the lines in order to spill it in just such a situation. Then Celestra laughed. "Oh, who am I kidding. I don't believe in their stupid cause."

Allegra sat forward. "Then tell us what is going on."

Celestra shook her head violently. "You don't understand. They will kill me if I talk."

Allegra took a breath. "They will kill you if you talk?" she asked, her tone hard.

Celestra nodded, her eyes shining with tears.

Allegra bent her head so she could meet Celestra's eyes. "And they will kill you even if you don't talk."

Her statement was met with utter silence. Celestra swallowed hard. Her gaze flickered to Max who sat silently on the other side of the coffee table, his expression indecipherable. Allegra knew he must be shocked but was playing the part of supporting her. She'd failed to tell him what she was going to say, but truth be told she'd had little idea herself until that very moment.

Celestra let out a low sob. "No. They promised they won't hurt me." She shook her head desperately, smiling through her tears as she looked at Allegra. "They promised."

"It doesn't matter what they promise," said Allegra, hating that she was forced to play the bad person. "Nothing they have told you matters, Celestra, because they *are* going to kill you."

"No." The words were the softest whisper and then she surged to her feet. She stalked toward the door. "No. I know what you're doing. You're jealous of Max and me. You just want to stake your claim, push me away. You want me out of the way so you're going to make me talk so you can throw me to the wolves."

She stopped in her tracks and rounded on Max, staring at him through a sheet of tears. "This is low. Even for you."

"Les, you have to listen to us. Your life is in danger."

Again, she shook her head, letting out a bitter laugh. "And you really expect me to believe that?" Though the words were filled with bravado, a tiny quaver in her voice gave her away. She was curious, and perhaps even the tiniest bit convinced.

Max got to his feet. "If you have even the slightest bit of self-preservation then you will listen."

"And if you have even the slightest bit of concern for the safety and well-being of the ambassador and his wife, then you will listen." Allegra hadn't realized she'd spoken the words until they were already out of her mouth.

Max gave her an odd look, but he didn't appear to want to stop her.

Allegra walked toward Celestra. "I'm sorry to be so hard on you, and I know you're scared, but it's not just about you or me any longer. The whole city is in terrible danger."

"Don't you think I know that?" Celestra shook her head, her voice rising until it cracked. "I wish I could do something, but I don't want to end up dead." She began to cry, soft whimpers that touched Allegra's heart and brought a light sheen of moisture to her own eyes.

Allegra took a shaky breath and glanced over at Max. He gave her a barely perceptible nod. She took another step toward Celestra, stopping in front of the girl. "You *are* going to end up dead."

CHAPTER 14

*A*llegra's harsh words stopped the soft sobs, and Celestra's head rose as she glanced at Allegra, shock widening her eyes.

Allegra continued, "Whatever it is you are trying to do, obeying every command because they are threatening you with death . . . it doesn't matter because there are going to kill you." Allegra half reached out to the terrified woman, but she stopped midway, retrieving her hands and holding them tightly at her waist.

Celestra was silent, and when Allegra glanced curiously at her, she found the woman was staring at Allegra's hands, a look of pure grief on her face. Slowly her gaze shifted away from Allegra's hands and settled on her face.

"What did you see?" she asked so softly Allegra would have thought she'd imagined it had she not seen Celestra's mouth move.

Allegra put an arm around the woman and drew her to the sofa. She had to force herself not to flinch when her fingers touched the bare skin on Celestra's arms. Thankfully she wasn't hit with a second vision.

Then she stiffened.

No. Not thankfully. No more visions likely meant Celestra was dead for sure, no matter what they did to avoid the circumstances that could have led to the death Allegra had seen in her vision.

The thought weighed heavily on Allegra's heart, but she walked Celestra to the sofa and sat her down, taking a seat beside her.

"Tell me."

"I don't—"

"Please tell me."

"Okay, I'll tell you. But you have to tell us whatever you can about these people. We have to do whatever it takes to stop them."

Celestra sniffed and nodded, taking a tissue from the box that seemed to magically appear in front of her. She gave Max a grateful glance, and he smiled and put the box on the coffee table.

All done, she met Allegra's eyes. "I need to know."

Allegra inhaled deeply then let the breath out. "I saw you in your room. You were on the bed."

Celestra stiffened, staring hard at Allegra's face. "My room?" She seemed to be asking Allegra more than what her words were.

Allegra nodded. "I'm not sure. The place was pretty run-down. But I saw your dress hanging on a hanger on a rack beside the bed."

"My dress?"

"The long white one. With the patterns . . ." Allegra waved at her ankles indicating the hem pattern on the white dress.

Celestra nodded.

"Is that where you live?"

Another nod. "You say they . . . it happened there?"

"Yes. In my vision, I saw your body after . . ."

"So, you didn't see it happen?"

Allegra shook her head. It was a good thing too. "You'd taken a pretty bad beating."

"They beat me to death?" Her voice shook again.

Allegra nodded unsure of whether it made any sense to tell the woman all the terrible details.

She cleared her throat. "Can you think of what would have sent them over the edge? So far, you've toed the line with them, so what could have made them decide . . ." Allegra fell silent unsure of how to continue the questioning.

Thankfully, Max took over.

Allegra was grateful he'd let her take the lead on the questioning, and she was glad she no longer needed to. She'd much rather be watching or listening than to be the one actually doing the interrogation.

"I can get you to safety. You just need to be willing to do it."

"How can you possibly do that?" She shook her head. "What if they find out what we're doing?"

"I can get you recalled to the States, have your job role changed in such a way that it will not be under your own control, so they won't think you are a risk factor for them."

She was still shaking her head when Max finished speaking. "They have spies everywhere. They know every move I make." She gave a soft laugh. "If I hadn't first verified the building was empty I would bet they'd know I was here with you now. I made sure I had a good cover with the visa paperwork but still . . ."

"Tell me how it started."

She shook her head and began to fidget. "Does it really matter?"

"Yes. It'll help us figure out their pattern, maybe how they operate."

She sighed deeply. "After you and I . . . after we were over, I took the job with Senator Calvinius but eventually this position came up. It meant I could get away from everything and it sounded like . . . like an adventure." She glanced up at Max. "It was good for me. But they got to me early."

"How?"

"The best way to a girl's loyalty is through her heart." Her laugh was cold and self-deprecating. "I was lonely, and they played me. A man approached me, young and handsome and charming. I fell for it. Eventually, he introduced me around, and I became part of a larger circle. I thought I had friends . . . a place I could call home."

"They use the long game. It says they are patient. In no rush for whatever it is they have planned."

She nodded. "Then one day they took me to the mountains to see a man. I never saw his face . . . they blindfolded me all the way there and back."

"Right. BAO is nearby," murmured Max.

"BAO?" asked Allegra.

"Base of Operations," said Max and Celestra in unison.

Allegra nodded. "What did the man want?"

Celestra stiffened. "My complete loyalty or my lover would be killed."

"And did they keep their word? Or was he involved."

Celestra snorted. "Of course, they didn't. He was in on it. The bastard." She sighed. "I was played big time. I saw that not too long after I met the kingpin. Olivio changed . . . he became harder. At first, I thought he was under pressure with his life on the line. But eventually, I realized it was his true nature. Everything else about him had been an act to win me over."

Allegra sat forward. "You can't blame yourself."

"I can. I was blind and stupid."

"No. They are the ones to blame. You did nothing wrong. People play with each other's emotions all the time. Even in loving relationships. It's part of human nature. And when people like Olivio and his gang decide to prey on an innocent there is no knowing about it. They are predators, and it's not your job to know they are out to get you. Yes, you need to be aware and careful. Yes, you shouldn't be reckless. But with people like these . . . well, they are too good at what they do. Had it been me or even Max? It would have likely gone down the same way. Seduction, bribery, abduction . . . they would do whatever it takes to get what they wanted."

Max nodded and patted Celestra on the back in an almost awkward show of comfort. Allegra wondered if he'd have done better had she not been in the room.

He leaned toward Celestra. "I'm going to speak to a few people back home . . . see if I can pull a few strings and get you moved back." He paused as if considering something else. "I want you to just quietly disappear, so you don't tip anyone off."

She nodded. "We'll have to tell the ambassador though. Surely he'd need to know?"

Allegra and Max both shook their heads. "No," said Max. "If he is involved he could tip them off. We need it to be a clean removal."

"How will she get out of the country?" asked Allegra. "Won't they have people at the airports? If they are so well connected then they'd know as soon as she booked a flight out."

Max nodded. "I think I can get her a different passport. We are FAPA after all."

Both women smiled at that and Allegra sat back feeling slightly relieved. Celestra too appeared calmer now, but Allegra was worried. Celestra had spent such a long time under their control. Who knew how affected she had become by their doctrines. There was a slight chance she could have been converted to their thinking. There was also a slight chance Celestra was playing them right that very moment.

Celestra sighed and got to her feet. "I'd best be going. I'd rather not make anyone suspicious."

Max nodded, and he and Allegra got to their feet too. Max walked to the door, but Celestra stopped and turned to Allegra.

"Thank you," she said. "I'm very grateful to you. You didn't have to help me."

Allegra wanted to tell her it wasn't about Celestra at all. That nothing she or Max were doing was for Celestra or McIvor. It was all a means to saving an entire city from total destruction.

Instead, she smiled as Celestra gave her an awkward nod. Then the woman turned and was gone, refusing Max's offer to walk her out or help her get home. Perhaps she didn't want Max to see how she lived, or perhaps there was something more sinister going on.

There was nothing to do but wait.

CHAPTER 15

*E*xhausted, Allegra finally made it to bed, falling heavily onto the mattress with a groan that resonated somewhere between pleasure and agony.

She fell asleep almost instantly.

THE AIR IS WARM, and has a dry and dusty taste to it. Sounds drift toward Allegra's ears, but they echo and waver on the air as if drifting in from a distance.

When Allegra opens her eyes the bright sun almost blinds her, sending a sharp stab deep into her brain. She flinches, squeezes her eyes shut and waits as the throbbing fades.

Moments later she opens them again slowly.

This time she cracks her lids open and stares at the room around her through shuttered lashes. She sees dusty white stone walls and a rough ceiling which appears hand-plastered, the finish rough and uneven in places.

Slowly her eyes adjust to the glare, and she tries to sit up, knowing instantly that something is wrong.

Though her mind urges her body to move, it seems her limbs are functioning on a level beyond her own control.

Overlaid upon her thoughts are those of another person, someone who is more in control than Allegra is.

Her mind feels split in two, a separate awareness who is sure and calm, and much stronger in mind than Allegra. The other consciousness overshadows Allegra's mind, a mind now terrified because she knows with absolute certainty she is no longer in control.

Oddly, she finds herself aware too that this feels more like a vision. Her first assumption had been that this was one of her many visions, a terrible prophetic window into a future she'd rather not see.

It is easier to believe this strange episode is a dream. And with everything she's been through in recent weeks, her most basic instinct demanded she follow the path before her to see where it leads.

Perhaps there is a path she must follow before she understands the true meaning of this vision.

She pays closer attention now as she finds herself rolling over, feeling the thin mattress shift beneath her as she gets to her feet. A woman enters the small sleeping quarters. She wears a simple white shift dress, her feet shod in slim leather sandals, giving Allegra the impression she is house-staff. She carries an earthenware jar and a deep bowl which she sets on a table beside a small square window. She pulls apart the drapes before hurrying out without a word.

No glass covers this window, and the only protection from the elements outside are two faded lengths of fabric masquerading as drapes. They hang over a long piece of string nailed into the stone above what is essentially an uneven hole in the wall.

Allegra—or rather the woman about whom she is dreaming— performs her morning ablutions and begins to untie her hair. She runs her fingers through her waist-length red tresses and begins to comb out the knotted locks.

There are no mirrors in the room, and from her current surround- ings, Allegra is already assuming she is not dreaming of the modern world. This is a time from the past, a window into the life of someone long dead, rather than of something still to happen.

The thought scares Allegra as she begins to wonder if she is in any danger from this strange dream state.

Still, when nothing happens over the next few minutes to threaten her life, she calms down and begins to pay closer attention.

Though the sleeping quarters are simple, the home itself is fairly large and well-appointed. Plants in large earthenware pots dot the halls, and here and there the floor is decorated with pieces of colored pottery, and unusual mosaic tile.

The woman goes deeper within the house, emerging into a small courtyard where a quartet of sentries stand waiting. Their skins gleam, tanned dark in the hot sun, and yet they remain there unmoving. They are wearing the uniform of soldiers, brass breast-plates, plumed helmets, and armor.

Between them sits a large shaded seat set on poles, and Allegra understands these men are here to transport her elsewhere.

A word echoes in her mind. Lectica. She assumes this refers to the litter the men are standing beside.

Whoever this woman is, she appears to be powerful and respected. At least powerful enough to have soldiers perform her transport requirements.

Allegra's host climbs inside the lectica and seats herself without a word. The sentries bear the woman through the front gates of the compound and down a hillside.

They walk sedately through a bustling town, skirting a market filled with shouting and laughter, filled with the lowing of cows and the bleating of goats and the screaming of children.

As they go, people stare, and some come closer, calling out to the woman. Allegra doesn't hear what they say, but it is of a concern because being this close to the unknown makes her aware that when she wants to go back home, it may not be as simple as merely opening her eyes and waking up.

The sentries walk through the town and up another hillside where they stop at a pair of giant doors set into a stone wall. The walls run around another compound and Allegra finds herself holding her breath during the wait for the doors to open.

She isn't sure what she'd expected, but it is certainly not Delphi.

Up on the hills before them sits the Temple of Delphi, and Allegra's heart twists both with fear and with joy.

Is this really a dream? Or is it perhaps a memory from a Pythia long dead?

Allegra forces herself to stop speculating and concentrate on the sentries as they come to a stop and lower the seat. She feels a little queasy as the four men rock the lectica as they kneel and set it carefully onto the ground.

She supposes there is a first time for everything, and she's just experienced her first time being carried around in a chair on the shoulders of four strong men.

As Allegra studies the compound, she catches sight of a group of toga-garbed men drawing closer, speaking hurriedly in low tones, their eyes furtive as they glance Allegra's way.

Though she tries to listen in, she finds their language —though familiar—difficult to fully comprehend. She hadn't expected to understand the Ancient Greek tongue, but she begins to find that if she listens through the woman—who Allegra had begun to refer to in her mind as her Host—then she is able to better understand the men.

It takes some getting used to, but she eventually absorbs the understanding and soon she is no longer listening and translating using the woman's knowledge. Instead, she is simply knowing.

The woman steps off the chair, accepting the help of the sentries with an easy grace, and Allegra finds herself walking up a slight incline toward the gathered men.

Many are smiling as she draws abreast of them, but though they wish her good morning, she merely nods and waves, and continues walking.

As Allegra passes the men, one particular face stands out, so familiar and yet she cannot put a finger on where she'd seen him before.

Though she struggles to remember, she has little time to spend on it as the woman continues walking and is soon out of sight of the men. Allegra is certain, from their bearing and dress that they are senators.

That begs the question as to who the woman is that Allegra has hitched a ride within. She is at the mercy of the woman's physical movements, and suddenly Allegra has an overwhelming need to go back to her own consciousness.

Panic strikes her, and she finds herself growing lightheaded again.

Is it perhaps all just a truly strange dream?

That chocolate had been too good to be true...had there been something in it?

But as she moves with the woman, as she feels the sun on her skin she knows it's more than just a dream.

She begins to feel that it is some sort of strange astral projection, only one that has taken her back in time.

To the era of a very different Pythia.

The woman makes her way up the hillside and passes a number of smaller buildings before she reaches the main temple.

The Temple of Apollo at Delphi.

The multitude of columns, the large triangular pediment, the long rectangular building. A stunning piece of architecture she is seeing in its own time, an opportunity she is sure is not a common one.

So many of Apollo's temples had been destroyed during a particularly horrible period in history during which almost every Apollonian place of worship in the world had been badly damaged. The only other time in her life she'd seen an Apollo temple intact was when Apollo himself had taken her away from her torture at the hands of Lord Langcourt, the High Priest of the Order of Hermes. The god had transported her to another place and likely another time, in which she'd seen a temple of Apollo in all its glory.

Allegra now knows what she is witnessing. If it is a dream, it is one of such fine detail that she suspects she would recall most of the specifics when she awakens.

Allegra hurries up the incline and begins to climb the stairs leading up to the temple. She moves from bright sunshine into shadow, and yet she doesn't feel any cooler. Formidable marble columns rise high, holding up the long rectangular roof structure of the temple.

Surrounded by a forest of columns, Allegra feels the weight of the building bearing down on her. She walks up the front portico, along the pronaos toward the inner sanctum of the temple. At the far end sat Naiskos, the inner, true temple of Apollo. But Allegra takes the steps down into the hall, then continues further into the Adyton, or the Oracle room.

This is where the Pythias had spoken their predictions all those centuries ago. Allegra finds she knows so many things without knowing, and wonder fills her so greatly she feels lightheaded.

But she isn't allowed a respite. No, the woman within whom Allegra now travels seems determined to perform her duty and appears to be unaware of Allegra's presence.

Which Allegra thinks is strange considering she can read the woman's thoughts so clearly. The woman—and Allegra—enters the sanctum where a priestess in the far corner busies herself with lighting the flames of a number of torches.

Two narrow cracks run along the ground, and crisscross each other. At their meeting point is a wider, well-like depression over which sits a tripod chair.

"Cathenna," a voice tugs Allegra's attention away from the sight of the inner sanctum of the Oracle's temple. She glances up to see the senators enter, like a gaggle of fat white geese.

Allegra blinks. Where had that thought come from?

Somewhere within her consciousness, Allegra smiles. Cathenna. A wave of sadness fills Allegra at the thought that this could really be just a dream. It would be a sad thing to awaken later, only to find it has all been merely her overactive imagination thrusting these beautiful visions upon her.

Cathenna waits as the group—or gaggle—of men hurry closer.

"My Lady, we were hoping for a few minutes of your time." The man at the head of the gaggle comes to a sudden stop three feet from the

Oracle, his rounded cheeks flushing, his little beady eyes sparkling. He seems secretly amused by something. Or perhaps that is just his expression.

"How may I assist, Senator?" Cathenna's voice surprises Allegra, as for a moment she'd forgotten she is using the woman like a vehicle.

"We require Apollo's word. At your earliest convenience, of course." He tacks on the last sentence and Allegra is certain he means none of it. Despite his cheery demeanor, Allegra suspects the sparkle in his eye is more venom than pleasantry.

Cathenna is shaking her head and Allegra tenses. These men don't appear to be the type easily refused. Allegra studies the group and catches sight of the man who'd seemed familiar to her when she'd first seen the senators.

Allegra's heart tightens, her vision beginning to blur.

Langcourt.

The high priest who'd tortured Allegra is standing not three feet from her. Almost two thousand years in the past.

Allegra takes a deep shuddering breath and suppresses the urge to laugh. Not Langcourt, but perhaps someone related to him.

The feeling of lightheadedness doesn't abate, and Allegra struggles to focus.

Langcourt's double could just be a huge coincidence. People did have doppelgängers, so perhaps Langcourt's just happens to exist two millennia in the past.

Allegra's vision begins to blur as she stares at the man. Her gut is telling her something she doesn't want to hear.

And before she could sift through her emotions, she found her eyes opening to a different type of sunshine.

To the cooler, wetter, more tropical warmth of Qusqu.

CHAPTER 16

*A*s exhausted as he was, Max found he was unable to fall asleep. He tossed and turned, and ended up twisted up within the sheets. Kicking them off, he got to his feet and went to the window.

Sliding the glass open, he stared out at the night sky, listening to the music of a multitude of insects and other nocturnal animals. Crickets and cicadas chirped, and a night parrot called to its mate. Somewhere in the distance, a jaguar roared, warning the humans that he still owned the night.

Overhead, the stars were sprinkled against a blue-black sky glittering like diamonds.

The universe, those stars, none of what lay out there in the Milky Way could ever know the troubles humanity faced, because humans fought not only their fellow man, but waged war within themselves.

Sometimes Max had reason to wonder what the point of it all was.

Here he was, fulfilling a lifelong dream, doing his duty, serving the Pythia, and he was faced with an inner turmoil that refused to remain in the shadows.

Seeing Les so broken had hurt him more than he'd expected. They'd had something special, a long time ago. He still cared for her, of course. Max had never been a careless man. He'd never been in an empty relationship either.

And Les knew very well why they'd parted.

It was probably why she'd been so curt at first. He'd seen the look in her eyes the moment he'd walked through the front doors of the embassy building. Shock had darkened the blue of her eyes, and had been replaced with anger. Only temporarily, of course.

Max knew Les was more angry at herself than she was at him. She'd been unable to handle his loyalty to the Pythia. That he'd jet off to see her at a moment's notice had never sat well with Les.

She'd only understood when Aurelia had predicted an oil refinery explosion they had been too late to prevent. Celestra had realized then how important his relationship with Aurelia was, but it had been too late for them as a couple.

Max worked purely on trust.

A trust he had broken in his dealings with Allegra. One he'd hoped to have mended. But that too had been too late.

Max sat on the chair behind him, finding himself bathed in moonlight. He thought back to the day he'd first met Aurelia. At fourteen, Max had been smart mouthed, arrogant and stubborn as hell.

Walking past a coffee shop, he'd bumped into an old woman. She'd almost fallen over, and he'd grabbed a hold of her hand, helping her back into her seat before he'd moved on. She'd smiled so brightly at him he'd thought her senile.

He'd walked on, meeting his friends at a local playground to hang out for a while. The old lady had sat on the bench at the edge of the field, waiting until he was done.

After some internal deliberation, he decided that going over to ask her what she wanted couldn't hurt. If she propositioned him, he'd turn her down politely.

Other than that, he wasn't sure what she could possibly want from him?

She beckoned him closer as he walked toward her, and he had no choice but to go to her. She patted the bench beside her. "Sit, my dear boy. Please sit. We have much to talk about."

Max had a hard time preventing himself from laughing, but he managed. Barely.

When Aurelia began to talk he'd become convinced she was crazy.

"Young man, you are so much more important than you know," she said, her voice quivering.

Max remained silent, waiting for her to continue. It was apparently the right thing to do.

"You are a rare breed my boy. And I mean that literally." She bent to look him in the eye. "Do you know how important you are?"

Max shrugged.

"One day you will come to work with me," she said with a wide grin. "You are the one. I touched you . . ."

The longer she spoke the stranger she began to sound, and a few minutes later, after hearing her go on and on about touching him, Max got to his feet, unnerved and more than a little creeped out.

"Don't go. I think I've scared you."

"I'm not scared."

"Pssht. It's good to be scared. Keeps the blood in your veins warm."

Max didn't know how to respond to that, so he chose to remain silent. That evening he'd acted out of instinct, and it seemed he'd done everything right.

Aurelia rambled on for a few minutes talking about testing, and prophecies. Max smiled at the incongruity of it all. Him of all kids, hanging out with a woman who seemed a little off-kilter.

He'd been the sports star, the athlete, the guy all the girls want, and who all the guys want to be. He'd also been a right little prick, an arrogant asshole who now, when he looked back, he hadn't the right to be.

He'd been so full of himself, and yet Aurelia had looked past it all. As much as she'd been old and cranky, she'd also been understanding and patient.

"You think you're special, don't you?" she'd asked, her gaze boring into him.

He stammered, becoming angry that she made him so uncomfortable.

"Well, you are special. Just not in the way you expected. Or probably not even in the way you want." Her smile was sly, as if she enjoyed being the one in control.

Max leaned back, arms folded. "Special how?" he asked, partly angered, mostly curious. What teenage boy could resist information on how special he is?

"You are Immunis," she said, her voice breaking on the word as she looked away.

Max frowned. "What's an Immunis?" he asked leaning forward. "What's so special about it?" The name had sounded intriguing, but the old woman was yet to reveal what made it so important.

She turned her gaze slowly back to Max, her rheumy eyes becoming clearer for a moment. "You are unique. In all the world, there is only one of you. And you are vital to me and to my kind."

"Your kind?" Max felt a trickle of trepidation along his spine. What was her kind? Was she some sort of alien or something? Max had heard about the claims that there were aliens in the universe.

Or she could just be one of the Gifted; the seers, the telepaths and others who had begun to reveal their powers.

Or she could be on some kind of recreational drug for the elderly. Or she could just be plain senile. There were too many possibilities.

At last, she said, "Do you know what an oracle is?"

He nodded.

"What about a Pythia?"

He rolled his eyes. "If you don't know about the Pythia you may as well be dead." He studied her for a moment. "Do *you* know the Pythia?"

The old woman smiled. "Perhaps I ought to have introduced myself." She twisted slightly in her seat, so she was facing him head on. Then she held out her hand. "My name is Aurelia Julian."

Max's jaw dropped as he stared at the old woman. "*You're* the Pythia?"

She nodded, her smile now sad.

"But shouldn't you have security? Like bodyguards or protection?"

"Why?"

"Because if people knew who you were when you walk by them on the street, they wouldn't leave you alone." He looked around, checking if anyone nearby could have overheard their conversation. But he found they were alone in the park, not a soul in sight.

Relieved he sat back. "Don't you care that they'd find out."

She shook her head. "Not at all. They don't see me. I'm old and unimpressive. Most people will walk straight past me."

Max hesitated. He'd been about to say he hadn't. But the truth was he'd only stopped because he'd wanted to prevent her from falling. And only because he'd been the one to bump into her in the first place.

Had he not almost knocked her over, he probably wouldn't have seen her either.

Aurelia grinned, and a line of faded white teeth gleamed at Max. "It's understandable. It is what I prefer. The anonymity is refreshing. I can move amongst the people without being disturbed. I've spent so many years in my life serving them they've forgotten I am still human, just like them."

Max understood what she meant, but he still wasn't sure what it had to do with him. His face must have revealed his doubt because Aurelia patted his hand. "Very well. I will no longer keep you in suspense." She smiled and sat against the back of the bench. "Do you know how the oracles see?"

Max nodded. "You touch a person, and then you can see their future."

"Yes. It's why I try not to touch people even if by accident."

"Why not?"

"Because there is the issue of privacy. Some people do not want to know what their future holds. Most people will only come to me if there is a good reason. There is only a certain type of person who wants a window into their future."

"I think I know what you mean. Those who have something to gain by it."

"Very good. You catch on fast."

Then Max froze. "But I touched you. When I bumped into you." His eyes rounded as he stared at Aurelia. "Did you see my future?"

Aurelia shook her head, her smile filled with what Max could only interpret as joy. "I didn't. And that is why you and I are here having this talk."

"Because you didn't see my future when you touched me?" Max didn't want to admit it, but he was so confused.

Aurelia got to her feet. "That is what it means to be Immunis. You are immune to the Seer's touch." She faced Max and smiled down at him. "You, my dear boy, are destined to be the Voice of the Pythia."

Max frowned, rising to his feet as a ripple of fear ran through his body. This was insane. The Voice of the Pythia? "I thought they were just a myth," he said, the words falling from his mouth before he realized what he was saying.

"A myth as much as the Pythia?" asked the old woman with a smirk.

Max bit the inside of his cheek as he considered his next move. "So, what is it you want from me?" he asked softly. He found it strange that he'd taken it so well. He hadn't lost his sanity. Or at least he hoped he hadn't.

Aurelia straightened and held out her hand. Max sensed she was asking him to offer his arm and he did. Good thing his father had insisted he learn how to behave in polite society.

"Walk me to my car, young man. We need to make arrangements for your training. And I will need to speak to your parents."

From there, everything had gone faster than he'd expected. At first, his parents had been shocked, first having to assimilate the existence of the Immunis, and then to accept their son was one of them. His father had bargained with Aurelia, insisting Max enter the military after his training with her.

The old woman had assured him that the training at the military academy would be easily surpassed by what she expected of Max. He'd been trained as a soldier, as a bodyguard, as a sniper, and an interpreter. He'd had to brush up on his Ancient Greek as Aurelia sometimes spoke her prophecies in the dead language.

Now he sighed as he stared at the stars again, well aware they were close enough to Aurelia's burial place so Allegra could perform a pilgrimage of sorts.

He got to his feet and headed for the bed, fatigue, at last, pulling heavily onto his body.

His last thought as he fell asleep was that even though he'd told Allegra the truth, he hadn't told her everything.

He'd have to do it soon, or it would be another strike against his name. He wasn't sure how she would take it. Even he had been shocked when Aurelia had told him.

The old woman had taken particular delight in imparting the shocking truth.

He remembered her words as if she'd spoken it yesterday. "There is one more responsibility of the Immunis, my boy. But don't worry. This does not apply to me. I believe I'm a little too old for you." She'd chuckled, as if enjoying her own little secret.

Max had frowned at the statement, a tension coiling within his stomach as he began to suspect what she was about to say.

"Through the ages, the Oracle's Immunis—especially because he is immune to her prophetic touch—has served as more than translator. More than just companion."

She'd smiled, her lips curling in a smirk.

"The Immunis will also be husband to his Pythia."

CHAPTER 17

*A*llegra groaned as she turned over. Her head felt heavy and wooly, as if she was suffering from a really bad hangover. She smashed her face into the pillow and sighed, stretching out her tight muscles.

Fatigue still pulled on her limbs and her eyes felt like she'd bathed them in sand. She'd been so exhausted last night that she'd been desperate for sleep.

Allegra stiffened.

She'd been dreaming. A strange, almost unbelievable dream, one she could—even now, in her waking consciousness—recall in vivid detail. Allegra pushed off the pillow and sat up, shoving her hair out of her face. She rubbed her forehead, wincing as the pressure only made her eyes feel worse.

She opened her eyes the tiniest bit, the narrow space between her lids sufficient to see the bright sunlight streaming into the room. Just fabulous. Perfect weather guaranteed to spoil a girl's morning.

Crawling out of the bed she stumbled into the adjoining bathroom and washed her face, hoping the cool water would help wake her up. She felt only slightly better after brushing her teeth.

She reached for her hairbrush, intending to run it through her hair, but slowly froze to stare at her reflection in the mirror.

Her morning routine bore an uncanny similarity to that of Cathenna, the Pythia she'd visited in her dreams. Allegra blinked then shook the thoughts from her head. Everyone's routine on waking would be similar; only so many steps to consider.

At that moment, she heard a door open and close, confirming Max was also awake.

She threw on her wrap and headed out to talk to him. She had a lot to tell him, and she couldn't wait to see his face when she described her dream-vision.

"LANGCOURT HAS A DOPPELGÄNGER?" asked Max, his eyes hooded and dark after listening to her tale. Throughout her monologue he'd remained in total silence.

"Is that all you got?" asked Allegra. "Cathenna? The Temple of Apollo? Delphi? All unbelievable and fascinating and yet *your* focus is on the doppelgänger?" She shook her head, not sure if she should be amused or annoyed.

Max grinned and nodded. "Of course. What else could my focus be? Pythias are a dime a dozen," he said airily. "Now doppelgängers of mass-murdering-Pythia-torturing killers? *They* aren't common."

Allegra laughed, taking a sip of her chocolate. "You're calling me common, are you?" She felt a little more relaxed now, especially after spilling all the details of her dream to Max.

Max shrugged in answer, his expression a little distant. Then he looked over at Allegra, his expression grim. "This vision you've had . . . whatever it is you've seen . . . it would be easy enough to dismiss as just a dream. But you must remember who you are."

Allegra frowned. "So you think the dream is real?"

"I don't know. You saw a Pythia in her time, two thousand

years ago. It's easy to assume you were dreaming. It's also easy to accept it would be real. There is no way to definitively know until it happens again." Max nodded to himself as he spoke. "You saw someone who looked like Langcourt. That could just be your subconscious worried about where he'd disappeared to, and what his connection is with the Pythias before you."

Allegra nodded and got to her feet. She headed over to the window and stared out at the mountains in the distance. "I know. A part of me knows I can't expect the dream to have been real, but another part of me feels like there cannot be any other explanation of it. It feels wrong to negate it, to label it a dream and push it aside."

Max walked over to Allegra. "If you feel that strongly about it, then I think you should explore the dream a little more. Perhaps write it down in as much detail as you can and then you and I can go over it together."

Allegra looked at him, her eyes wide with surprise. "That's a quick turnabout."

"Not really. Not if you consider that only *you* know what the dream is about. Sometimes Aurelia used to channel visions and she'd only speak in Ancient Greek. Who knows? Maybe Aurelia was also seeing something from the past. What we can't do is ignore something that could be significant."

Allegra nodded, making a mental note to ask him for more details about Aurelia. He'd not been too forthcoming so far where it came to Aurelia. "What we can't do is ignore what we came here to accomplish." As she spoke the words she realized she'd all but forgotten about the disaster that would soon fall upon the city. "And now that we are allowed to stay, perhaps it's time to go have a look around."

Max nodded, then gave Allegra a narrow-eyed inspection. "Don't you think you'd be better off staying here?"

Here where it's safe, was what he really meant.

Allegra shook her head. "Not a chance. Besides, how would

you know what to look for if I'm not there to guide you? I'm the one with the memory of the place in my head." Max opened his mouth to protest but Allegra reached out and placed a finger on his lips. "Don't waste your breath fighting me. I'm going and that's that. I didn't come here to while away my time inside the room."

Allegra's monologue faded away as she realized where her finger was. Beneath her flesh she felt the soft curve of Max's skin, and suddenly, despite her distrust, she wanted to be near him, to feel his breath on hers, his arms around her body again.

Max's breath quickened, warmer now on the tip of her finger and Allegra retrieved her hand. The moment she broke contact she felt bereft of his warmth. And though they no longer touched, the awareness in the room remained, heavy and pulsing around them.

Allegra watched Max take a step closer to her and she willed him to take one more, her heart thundering as heat filled her body.

A rapid blast of knocking on the door shattered the vortex of emotions between them.

Startled, Allegra took a step back and forced her features into something she hoped resembled calm. If her cheeks were red though, she didn't have a hope of projecting serenity.

A late breakfast was being delivered but despite her hunger, Allegra wished the wait staffer had never come by.

The man set the food on the table beside the window and from the furtive glances he gave her she began to wonder if he'd come with the intention of seeing the Pythia rather than merely doing his job.

He met her eyes on the way out, and the ice in his expression was enough to confirm how he felt. Another thing to consider was the possible existence of a traitor within the ambassador's staff.

When the door closed, Allegra turned to Max. "We need to move on this as soon as possible."

"Yeah. I saw that." He was staring at the closed door, his eyes contemplative. "I suspect there is much more going on here than first meets the eye."

Allegra took a deep breath. "Right. Let's eat. I want to do some sightseeing as soon as possible."

CHAPTER 18

The people of Qusqu were a strange lot.

Langcourt stood on the shallow balcony halfway up the side of the pyramid, surrounded by a thriving jungle filled with green trees and exotic birds. Even in the middle of the day the call of the jaguar was not unusual. A wild place indeed.

One crying out to be tamed.

Langcourt considered the different tribes and states of the people he'd met since he'd arrived here two weeks ago.

The common folk were not the subservients you'd find back home in Brittanica. Here, where the emperor ruled with a brutal and bloody hand, the people were fiercely proud warriors who lived not in fear of their tyrannical king, but with a passionate loyalty that would put the head of anyone who challenged them in danger of ending up on a spike.

The High Priest Chief was going to pose a problem to Langcourt's plans. Their first meeting hadn't gone well. Not as far as Langcourt was concerned. While Roquefort busied himself with genealogies and Langcourt's agents scoured the earth for crucial information on the mysterious Pythia Allegra Damascus, Langcourt found himself at particular odds with the priest.

Of ancient tribal stock, the man was formidable, ruthless and entirely unpredictable. Perhaps it was Langcourt's inexperience with dealing with these almost-uncivilized people, but he found the experience distasteful.

Likely what added to his dislike was the sense of power Langcourt had felt running through the chief. What extra sensory perception the man possessed, Langcourt was none the wiser. Not that he planned to remain so. He'd already begun to investigate the man.

Had he not discovered the chief's plan he'd have negotiated easily enough and taken what he could get from the man. Now, things were different. He owed it to himself—if not humanity—to keep a closer eye on this high priest. Langcourt's concern now was not merely the power the man possessed, but the undeniable strength of it.

In his lifetime, Langcourt had crossed paths with hundreds, if not thousands, of abominations. The power they'd possessed had ranged from a flickering flame to raging fires. Sinchi was a volcanic eruption.

Far too much like the Pythia.

And that was the crux of the problem.

Here in Qusqu, Langcourt had found himself faced with two paramount problems, two abominations whose powers were fed by the innate strength of gods who had no business interfering in the lives of humanity.

Langcourt was not about to turn a blind eye. Nay, he'd spent so many years fighting these abominations that it would be insanity to ignore it right now. He'd come to find refuge, but his destiny always seemed to follow him.

His own purpose as the quencher of the flames of abomination seemed to have more control of his life than he himself did. And he wasn't complaining.

Now, all he had to do was to find out how to snuff out the

power feeding the chief's veins. How to access the god and sever the connection to the man.

Langcourt smiled and nodded to himself. He had a plan.

If the god didn't come to the man, then the man would go to the god.

CHAPTER 19

M ax suppressed a self-recriminating sigh as he motioned to Allegra to cross the road.

Allegra's revelation about her dream had set Max more on edge than he'd expected to be.

He suspected his discomfort was intertwined with the secrets he kept from her. He'd given her only a tidbit of detail regarding Aurelia, and he hadn't missed the curiosity in her gaze. To her credit she hadn't pushed him about his service to the previous Pythia, and he knew Allegra wasn't the type to pry even if she was owed that information anyway.

Which she was.

Max was just being unfair to her. His own feelings didn't matter in the greater scheme of things.

Max nodded to himself and focused on their next step.

Looking over his shoulder, he decided it was time to let Allegra in on the bad news.

He leaned closer and she complied, shifting toward him, her ear tipping close. He took a breath. "We are being followed."

Allegra's eyes widened for a moment, then narrowed as she studied Max's face. "For how long?"

She was beginning to get to know him too well. "Since we left the embassy."

She shook her head and followed him in silence as he headed inside a small market. Stalls were set up haphazardly, forcing tourists and shoppers to wander around seemingly aimlessly.

Max guided Allegra along, keeping up the pretense of taking the Pythia on a sightseeing trip. They moved past stalls piled high with colorful rugs and pillows, heading toward the busiest section: the food stalls.

The air was filled with the smells of cooking cornbread and spicy chicken. The aisles were thick with people waiting for their orders. The system was pay, get a token and move to a new line, so each stall had two sets of lines, taking the mayhem to second-level insanity.

Max touched Allegra's arm and pointed at a larger stall that had provided a long table at which their customers could consume their orders of flat cornbread filled with chicken strips, peppers, chili and a strange avocado paste.

Max ordered two, partly to satiate his taste buds—which had begun to water as soon as he'd gotten the smell—but mostly to keep up the pretense of sightseeing as the average tourist would.

Taking their tokens he led Allegra to the table, and leaned an elbow onto the roughly hewn wood, scanning the area for their two tails.

"Where are they," Allegra asked, giving him a cheery smile.

He glanced at her, and through an equally happy grin he said, "Two of them, tall, dark and dangerous."

"Exactly the way I like my men," murmured Allegra, her eyes flitting left and right.

Max gave her a sideways glance and let out a bark of laughter. She'd been on edge most of the morning but hadn't lost her quirkiness. His eyes drifted across her frame, taking in the long coffee-colored dress/coat and the brown leather pants beneath.

Despite the heat she'd worn brown leather boots as well, giving her a very badass, far-too-sexy look.

Allegra smiled back at him, her expression a little too cheeky for his liking. Was she flirting with him?

He didn't think so. Especially since he was yet to give her a proper explanation of the whole General Aulus debacle.

He was just about to tell her they needed to talk, when their order was called up and he had to leave her side to fetch it. He wasn't comfortable with leaving her all by herself and was beginning to think they should have organized additional security.

When he returned to the table, bearing two steaming hot cornbread rolls, he found Allegra attempting to fend off the attentions of a couple who'd managed to occupy the narrow space Max had just vacated.

Handing Allegra her food, he glanced at the two interlopers. "Is everything okay?" he asked, staring at them perhaps a little too long. He figured intimidation would work better than a physical attempt to get rid of them.

The woman, a little too blonde to be a native in these parts, leaned forward conspiratorially. "We know who she is, but don't worry. We won't tell."

Max raised an eyebrow, giving his roll a longing look. "So, who is she? This all sounds rather mysterious."

The woman pursed her lips, irritation plain in her eyes. "The Pythia of course. Do you not know who you're escorting around?"

Max took a bite, accepting the nosy woman wasn't about to leave them in peace anytime soon. After chewing and swallowing, he wiped his mouth off with the heel of his hand. "Are you telling me she's *the* Pythia? As in the Oracle woman?" He made a face, as if he found it hard to believe.

Then he looked over at Allegra, hoping she'd play the part.

"Are you really her?" he asked, his voice pathetic and totally in awe.

Allegra laughed. "Sorry, but no. As much as I wish I could tell the future, you've got the wrong girl."

The woman's mouth turned upside down and she gave her partner a sharp stab to the ribs with her boney elbow. "You said it was her," she hissed at him, her dark green eyes flashing with venom.

He held up his hands. "Hey, sorry if I was wrong. Coulda sworn it was her." His lips slanted in a strange smile, his eyes gleaming as he studied first Max and then Allegra.

The woman gave a hard grunt and spun on her heel, brushing past Max so hard he almost dropped his food. He shoveled the rest of it into his mouth, glad to see the back of the woman.

But something nagged at the back of his mind. Was it the woman? She'd certainly been obnoxious enough.

Max couldn't put a finger on it so he turned back and focused on Allegra. She'd also finished her food, and was squashing the wrapper into a small ball, giving her mouth the same treatment he'd given his. Their meal had come without paper towels and he made a mental note to carry some around with them wherever they went. Though the food was good, the all-round customer service was certainly not equal to the NGS.

Then he stopped himself. He wasn't usually this judgmental and he needed to stop. "We should go," he said leaning toward Allegra.

"Do you see them?"

"No. But that doesn't mean they aren't around. This is their territory. They'll blend in too well."

"So, does that mean today was a waste of time?"

He shook his head and offered her his arm. "I wouldn't think so. The day's not over yet."

"So where to next?" Allegra asked curling her fingers around his bicep as he began to track a steady pace through the crowd.

"We go—"

Allegra's fingers tightened on his arm and Max turned to check what was wrong.

Allegra was staring up at him, a strange confused expression on her face. For a moment, Max wondered what was wrong.

But then he saw the blotch of red on her chest. Red that soaked into the pale fabric and began to spread in a large bloodstain.

And then Allegra sank to the ground.

CHAPTER 20

*M*ax paced the stone floor in front of Allegra's room. Had there been carpets beneath his feet he'd have worn a line in it by now. The embassy doctor had been and gone, and though the man had been calm and sensitive, assuring Max that Allegra would be okay, and insisting he get some rest, Max had continued to wait for the other shoe to drop.

Why was it so hard for him to hope, or at least to be positive about Allegra's recovery?

Max was a hardened soldier. He'd seen three tours on the frontline, fighting in the African jungle and the depths of the Mongol horde, and even a small skirmish in a land on the other side of the world called Aotearoa.

Despite such bloody battles under his belt, the sight of Allegra's blood flowing from her body, coupled with her collapse, had rendered Max just about useless.

He'd at least been able to make the call to the embassy to call for help and an ambulance.

And then he'd sat on the dusty ground, surrounded by curious passersby, with Allegra cradled in his arms. He'd refused to let go, and had only allowed the doctor to take her from him when the man had reminded him she could die if Max didn't let him do his job.

Now, she lay unconscious on the bed, her skin pale, her golden hair combed and tucked to one side. Les had arrived an hour after the doctor had completed his surgical removal of the bullet from Allegra's chest, and had remained at Allegra's side.

It was a strange thing, watching the woman he had once loved, nurse the woman who was now his entire world.

He wasn't sure what he would have done without Les. She'd washed Allegra's skin, cleaning off the remaining bloodstains and soil. She'd combed through Allegra's hair and removed her makeup, then proceeded to bully Max into getting some sleep.

He'd obeyed more out of exhaustion than anything.

Now, he stood on the threshold of Allegra's room, leaning against the doorjamb, watching her as she slept.

"She's still unconscious," he said more to himself than anything.

"The doctor said not to expect an overnight recovery, Max. You need to take it one step at a time." Les was walking to him, a mug in her hand. "Coffee?" She held the mug out to him.

Taking the drink, he shifted his gaze back to Allegra's unmoving form. "She looks so vulnerable."

"Just because she's a powerful oracle doesn't mean she's no longer human." Les smiled. "Besides, she should look vulnerable. The bullet hit her half an inch above her heart. It missed the collar bone in the front and the shoulder blade in the back. No permanent damage. She's one lucky girl."

Max sighed, wrapping his fingers around the warm ceramic of the mug and taking a refreshing sip. "It's my fault. I should have been more careful. I got complacent."

Les shook her head, placing a hand on his arm. "Max, you can't blame yourself. This situation . . . Allegra knew what she was walking into. Don't diminish her efforts in this by making it your responsibility."

Max understood what Les was trying to do but he didn't agree. He should have at least added more security. "I shouldn't have let her convince me. I shouldn't have allowed her to go."

Les snorted. "I don't know Allegra very well, but more than her honesty—and even more than her need to help—it is her independence that impresses me the most. I don't see her taking orders from anyone. I have a feeling whatever you told her, she'd have done what she wanted to do in the end."

She smirked and took the now empty mug from his hand. He couldn't recall drinking any of it.

Max laughed. "That's a little true. She convinced me that she should go. But she's my responsibility. And with everything that's happening I should have been more careful." He turned to study Allegra again, his heart twisting at how vulnerable she looked.

Someone had shot at the Pythia. Someone had tried to assassinate the one person who could save the city from total annihilation. Whoever had hired the sniper had wanted Allegra dead. Yes, they had failed, but Max had to wonder what their end game was. What had they hoped to gain from her death?

Were they so afraid of her power that they would attempt to kill her?

Things in Qusqu were more dangerous than they'd thought.

A knock at the door pulled him out of his thoughts and he watched as Les headed over, her spine a little stiffer, as if she wasn't expecting anything good. She opened the door for the ambassador who gave Les a strange, slightly suspicious look, as if curious as to what she was doing in the Pythia's apartment.

Max didn't particularly care what the man suspected. He was sure McIvor could have easily discovered their past relationship, but Max wondered if that would actually benefit them by sending the man in the wrong direction. If he thought Max and Les were lovers again it would mean Les wouldn't be in so much danger from the people threatening her.

Max stepped away from Allegra's room and closed the door

softly. The last thing he was going to do was to make a spectacle of the Pythia while she was unconscious. Allegra would have his head if she found out.

"Commander, I came as soon as I heard. I'm so sorry," McIvor said as he reached a hand out to take Max's. His grip was firm and hard, as if for some reason he needed to establish his strength and believed a firm handshake would set the scene for the main show.

"Thank you, Ambassador. I'm sure the Pythia will appreciate your visit." Max nodded slowly, hoping McIvor wasn't going to stick around for too long. He didn't have the time or the inclination to put up with the man. Not when his mind was focused on Allegra.

McIvor smiled and nodded, his expression contemplative and sad. And completely false. "Elana sends her wishes. She'd hoped to come with me but she got tied up with work."

Max didn't believe that excuse for a second. In fact, he'd been curious as to the absence of the ambassador's wife. He knew she'd taken interest enough to send Allegra a dress as a welcome gift, and to look after her at the ball. He put Elana's absence on his list of things to investigate.

Now, he smiled as serenely as he could. "The Pythia will be most grateful."

McIvor took a step closer. "Commander, I have to be frank. In light of the attack on the Pythia, do you not believe it is in her best interest to return to the States where she will be safer?"

Max laughed. "I don't believe you know our Pythia very well. She has a mind of her own, Ambassador. She wouldn't listen to *me*, so do you really expect that she would listen to you?"

McIvor cleared his throat, shifting his attention away from the view and back to Max. "I'm just concerned, Commander. I do think it will probably be wisest for you to return the States. Perhaps the Pythia would find it better to recuperate where there are doctors at her disposal night and day." As he spoke his gaze shifted away from Max's face to focus again on the window and the view outside.

Max found it odd that the man hadn't asked to see Allegra. It would have been the natural request of someone who cared.

"I understand your concern, Ambassador, but the Pythia isn't the kind of person to hide herself away when she is needed. We are here for a reason, and I very much doubt the Pythia will leave without having achieved some part of what she'd intended.

"Whoever these people are who think they can intimidate her had better pray hard. Because we will come looking for them. And it won't only be the NGS that will put their full weight behind the investigation. The Pythia belongs to the world, and the world will want to know how this could have happened. The Qusquan government had better have a good reason for allowing this to happen."

"Surely you can't hold them responsible?" His eyes widened, sparking what to Max looked a lot like anger.

"Well, I do. And so will all the other countries who are part of the Treaty. They are already asking for the Qusquan officials to verify what security protocols were in place for her stay."

"Security protocols?" McIvor laughed. "The last thing the Qusquan government would have when it comes to the Pythia is security protocols. The Pythia isn't of much concern to General Qhapaq or the rest of the security departments." He spoke haughtily and Max frowned.

"Why, Ambassador McIvor, you sound defensive. Almost as if you agree with the Qusquan position. Is there any reason for us to question your loyalties to the NGS?"

McIvor paled and Max had to wonder who had decided that a position of diplomacy would be a good career choice for him. The man's expressions were right there for all to see. A particularly bad choice as a mole.

If that's what he was.

McIvor cleared his throat. "I don't appreciate your tone, Commander."

But Max shook his head. "I don't particularly care what you appreciate, Ambassador. All I know is someone out there wants the Pythia dead. And the Pythia came to Qusqu to investigate a possible mass destruction event. Now to me, that would make her a threat to those who are instigating—or who have knowledge of—such an event. And now she lies unconscious having come very close to being eliminated as a threat to these people."

McIvor turned away. "I'm not the enemy here, Commander. No matter what you may think, I am loyal to the NGS and I don't appreciate your . . . accusations." He looked at Max over his shoulder, his gaze shifting in Les's direction. "I do what I must, for my family's safety."

Max barely heard what the man said. His anger had risen, and simmered too close to the surface. He'd been upset over the shooting but seeing McIvor and seeing all these signs pointing toward the man being involved somehow, was about to put his fury over the edge.

Max snapped his gaze back to the ambassador's face. "And I do what I must for the safety of the Pythia. If I find even the slightest connection between you and these killers, I swear I will have you before the International Crime Council on charges of attempted murder."

"The ICC only hears cases against high-profile representatives of the people, like presidents and royalty. Surely you know that, Commander?" McIvor smirked, his lips curling, making Max want to shudder.

Max took a step closer to the man. "And what exactly do you think the Pythia is? She and her prophecies belong to the world. Besides, the last time I checked, the Pythia *is* considered royalty."

McIvor paled, his eyes darkening as he took a step away from Max. He opened his mouth, hesitating for a moment before saying, "I apologize, Commander. That was out of line."

Max didn't say anything. The fury in his eyes would have been enough of a response. At least now McIvor knew where Max stood. "Ambassador, I don't know what your relationship is to the people who are behind the Pythia's attempted assassination, but I assure you that should I find you are complicit in any way, I will hold you accountable."

McIvor shook his head, his face a study of emotion. Whatever his involvement, it was obvious he was conflicted about it. "I assure *you* that you are mistaken, Commander. The NGS and the safety of all our citizens in Qusqu are my highest priority. And I assure you the Pythia is at the top of my list."

Max gave the man a curt nod. He wasn't convinced but perhaps he ought to give him the benefit of the doubt.

McIvor headed for the door. Hand on the handle, he turned and looked over his shoulder at Max. "Commander, I know you aren't going to like my saying it, but I would like to reiterate that I do sincerely believe the Pythia will be safer in the NGS. The longer you and the Pythia remain here, the more dangerous it could be."

"Thank you for your concern, Ambassador. I will convey your opinion when the Pythia awakens."

Could the ambassador really be involved? And what exactly was his connection to General Qhapaq. That visit to the general's offices the day before could have been staged to intimidate Max, or perhaps get them away long enough to search their room.

McIvor nodded, then disappeared into the hall, leaving Max staring as Les closed the door, more concerned now than ever.

Still, it made no sense to Max. There was only one thing he knew for sure.

The ambassador's suggestion had sounded very much like a threat.

CHAPTER 21

*M*ax checked on Allegra to find her still asleep. He knew he couldn't expect her to wake up anytime soon, though he could still hope that she would.

Leaving her door ajar he headed to his room to grab his satellite phone. He never liked using it but this time it was necessary. His team back in the Capital would be waiting for him to touch base, especially since the last time he'd checked up on them had been almost a week ago.

He'd attempted to offer Aulus his resignation but the general had refused, insisting Max was capable of running the team from off-shore. Max knew the general was more interested in Max remaining at Allegra's side in order to maintain some form of influence over her.

He dialed and waited for Marcus—his second-in-command at the FAPA headquarters—to answer. Marcus Asante had taken over Max's old office, and was running the team in his stead. Max had suggested that he would adjust the roles so Marcus became Commander, but the man had insisted he was happy.

"When the shit hits the fan at least I know I'll be staying with you," he'd said.

"Commander," Marcus called out, his voice a little higher-pitched than normal due to the adjustments the sat phone made to the tones. "Good to hear from you, sir."

"Marcus, how are things at the Capital?"

The two men chatted about nothing for a few minutes, Max wanting to ensure Marcus was happy in his role as Acting Commander.

At last Marcus said, "You have good timing sir, there is something I need to tell you."

"Doesn't sound good," Max said, walking out of his room to check on Allegra. She was still fast asleep, a living sleeping beauty.

"It isn't. We've been keeping an eye on chatter regarding Allegra Damascus as well as the Pythia, and we've come across a few inquiries made regarding Allegra's birth and upbringing."

"Someone's looking into her past," murmured Max. "Do we have any clue as to who they are?" Max's mind was racing, wondering if someone here in Qusqu would be investigating Allegra's past.

"I have a team investigating, but unless someone has them on tape we have little chance of identifying them. We've had reports from birth registrations offices across the country. Good thing you said to flag her name as well as her family's. Pity the government offices don't have cameras. If we had a photograph of the perpetrators it would be easier, but we don't have much to go on."

Max considered the man's words. "Any surveillance images from The Britannic police? They would have done in-depth investigations into the members of the cult. Even the ones on this side of the ocean."

"Good idea, sir. You thinking the High Priest of that Hermes cult may have something to do with this?"

"It's possible. He may be missing but it doesn't mean he's dead, nor does it mean he's laying so low he'll ignore the Pythia altogether."

"Agreed. I'll put the team on it."

"What about our own attempt to suppress any details?"

"We're doing well. We are gathering the data, but I'm making sure it's kept top secret."

"Not even Aulus," said Max, his tone hard.

"I wouldn't have it any other way." Marcus knew all too well the complications of dealing with Aulus.

"He giving you any trouble?"

"The usual." Marcus was noncommittal, being the type of person to avoid gossip, especially where his superiors were concerned.

"I have another task for you," said Max, at last coming to the reason for his call.

"Shoot," Marcus said, his tone curious.

"I need you to pull up whatever you can on Ambassador Liam McIvor and his wife Elana, as well as Celestra Avesta."

"Les?"

"Yes. She's here in Qusqu. Secretary to the Ambassador."

"May I ask why we are investigating a friend?" Marcus' tone bordered on the critical, but Max understood. They'd all spent the better part of their twenties together, Max, Marcus, Celestra and a handful of others, a mix of FAPA agents and diplomatic staff.

"I think she's in over her head here. Possibly involved in something dangerous. In addition, can you investigate the possibility of getting her transferred back to the States ASAP? I'd be happy if she is on the next plane out."

"I can call in a favor or two. Can I call in a couple of your favors?"

"Absolutely. Whatever you need. You could say it's a matter of life or death."

"That bad?" Marcus sounded like a man who didn't want to hear this kind of truth even though he himself had asked the question.

"Worse."

"Very well, then." Marcus went quiet for a moment and Max imagined him writing notes. Then he asked, "What's the deal with the ambassador?"

"He's connected somehow. We're not entirely sure how, but he seems to be somewhat related to the people responsible for the destruction Allegra saw in her vision."

"You mean McIvor is a double agent?"

"I'd like to think not, but it's entirely possible. He's been very strange where it comes to our investigations. They're treating Allegra like a leper."

"Stupid of them," Marcus said, sounding irritated. "How is the Pythia anyway?"

"Hanging in there. She's asleep. We're hoping she'll come out of it soon."

"I still can't believe someone tried to kill her."

Marcus had been shocked when Max had called him earlier with the news of the attempt on her life. It had taken a while for the man to calm down, after which he had sworn that if he found the killers he cannot be held responsible for what he planned on doing to them.

All Max could think at the time was he'd have to get in line because Max himself would want to dispense the punishment,

Max rang off not long after, getting Marcus to go over the open cases the team had on the board. Though Marcus had insisted Max had other better things to think about, Max had still demanded the details.

It would be a good distraction. And it had been. Seeing his team busy and working, keeping his department running so well in his absence was uplifting.

Still, Max had a feeling it wouldn't last too much longer. At some point, he was going to have to make a choice.

CHAPTER 22

*N*othing.
Allegra opened her eyes and saw nothing.

More terrifying than any other vision she'd seen, more than any other horrific death, the absolute lack of everything was enough to turn her into an hysterical mess.

Breathe. She reminded herself to breathe, inhale, exhale, think. Where was she?

A soughing sound filtered to her, perhaps a soft breeze or a whistling of air through a narrow space. From around her came the echoes of voices in the distance, of the scraping of leather-shod feet against soft floors.

The sounds around her were familiar, as if she'd only just heard it, as if she heard them every day.

Allegra blinked.

SHE IS BACK in her dream about Delphi. The dream about the ancient Pythia Cathenna. Allegra blinks again and cast her searching gaze around the room, desperate to find her way through the shadows and out into the light. She would give even her last breath just to see one spark of light.

The nothingness is so much more terrifying than any horror a person could face. No wonder sensory deprivation is used as a form of torture. It will debilitate even the hardest of men.

Slowly her eyes adjust and she manages to make out the shapes of people around her. A blink later and the torchlight almost blinds her. It feels as if she's been pushed through a tunnel of darkness until she emerges into the light of Delphi.

Again, she seems to be inhabiting Cathenna's body, this she recognizes from the slim, tanned hands held out before her. Music plays somewhere in the distance, but here within the Oracle's chamber all occupants are silent as the night.

Around Cathenna, seven priestesses form a circle, as if a protective barrier. Beside Cathenna is an older man, his expression almost harsh as he studies the gathering beyond the circle of light.

An odd scent tickles Allegra's nose and she twitches her nostrils, suddenly becoming aware of a certain stiffness in the Cathenna's body. She doesn't want to assume anything, but she could have sworn the Pythia had felt a rush of emotion, of recognition.

It disappears quickly as the Oracle straightens, her attention moving to a group of men at her side. Their faces are lit by the torchlight, throwing an eerie light onto their features, hollows of eye sockets and cheekbones highlighted by yellow shivering flames.

They sit close by, watching Cathenna with a dangerous intensity, one Allegra had to wonder may pose a danger to the Oracle. Among the men is the doppelgänger of the high priest, his eyes piercing right inside Allegra's soul.

Or so it feels.

It takes only moments for Allegra to realize they are in the midst of summoning Apollo's words.

Back in the day, it was believed the word of the god Apollo was spoken through an Oracle. In more modern times, it was recognized that it wasn't truly the voice of Apollo, but rather the Oracle's own mani-fested power to access her visions.

Now Cathenna rocks back and forth and Allegra senses she'd partaken of some kind of calming drug. The man who stands beside her leans close, whispering something in her ear. Cathenna nods and then speaks in a language that most certainly is not Ancient Greek or Latin.

Frowning, Allegra wonders what is going on. Until the man beside her begins to speak, as if he's read the Oracle's words. Allegra studies the man. She knows what he is—a translator of the ravings of an Oracle, the man who tells each supplicant what the Pythia has said while within the grasp of the visions.

Minutes pass and the man speaks again, giving voice to what Cathenna has only mumbled. Allegra is still slowly settling into the dream and is yet to reach the point of understanding the language. But whatever the man has said, the gaggle seems satisfied.

Cathenna's mind seems adrift, and Allegra wonders if she's taken some sort of hallucinogenic drug. Or perhaps even a calmative. She tries to focus on the gathered audience and notices the gaggle has risen from their benches and are being led away by the priestesses attending Cathenna.

The translator steps over to Cathenna and helps her off the tripod chair. The Pythia's head lolls and she takes a deep breath.

"Can you stand on your own?" he asks her softly, his voice gentle as his gray eyebrows wobble.

Allegra feels a pull of emotion as the Oracle gazes at her translator.

So that's how it is.

The two are in some sort of relationship. The knowledge makes Allegra feel slightly voyeuristic. Cathenna nods and gives him a small smile. "I'm fine." She isn't really. Allegra can tell. From the feel of the scene and of Cathenna herself, Allegra has the sense that her current dream is placed much later along the timeline than the previous one.

She'd come to an understanding of the whole concept of the vision—that it is no dream, but rather a visit to the past via the Pythia bloodline.

Or something akin to that. It seems a more reasonable explanation than a mere dream. And should she believe such a wild theory, then it means there is a reason for her trip to the past.

She just has to figure out what that reason is.

Cathenna steadies herself and takes her translators arm, allowing him to lead her away from the Oracle's room and out into the Naiskos, the true temple of Apollo within the complex.

As Cathenna grows stronger on her feet, she lets the man's arm go and sighs with relief. "I hate that herb."

"I know," he murmurs, "But you must keep up the pretense. Nobody is to know that your visions are your own. Should they even discover that what you see is certainly not Apollo's message, you would no doubt suffer the consequences."

Another sigh. "I know. It is just difficult. I may be getting too old for this."

He moves to rub her back and she lifts her hand to stop him. Again, Allegra feels a rush of love for this man, and frustration ripples through her that she doesn't even know his name.

Thrasius.

Allegra hears the name as if it is a thought she's had on her own, as if she's read something aloud, and she is listening to the word echo within her mind.

She frowns—or tries to, and fails because Cathenna isn't frowning— and forces herself to remain calm and still. Is Cathenna communicating with her? If she is, then Allegra needed to pay closer attention.

She just isn't sure how to.

Cathenna's voice filters through to Allegra. "We must be careful Thrasius. The children . . ." Before Cathenna could continue, the gaggle descends upon the couple, all smiles. Following closely is a horde of revelers, drumming on small toubeleki and clanging on zill, the sharp sound made by the finger cymbals making Allegra flinch.

The crowd pushes against them and Thrasius tries to guide Cathenna aside, but they and the gaggle of senators are shoved along with the horde. Cathenna stumbles, tripping up a couple of revelers. In the confusion, Allegra loses sight of Thrasius. She feels a wave of fear from Cathenna and tries to send the other Pythia good thoughts.

A rush of gratitude fills Allegra and just as she begins to smile, fierce hot pain flares at the back of her ribs. Cathenna stills as she crouches, curving her body against the stampede feet.

Allegra tries to look around but she is limited to what Cathenna is looking at. Allegra focuses, finding her vision directed at a pair of sandaled feet a few yards to her left. Cathenna glances upward and as Allegra's vision fades she catches sight of two significant things.

A thin stiletto-bladed knife still glistening red with blood.

And the face of a man so familiar to Allegra that her stomach twists with the urge to throw up.

When blackness takes her, Cathenna whispers in her ear, "Beware, my child. Do not make the mistakes I have. He will come for you."

And then the darkness intensifies, becoming so opaque and so filled with nothing that Allegra screams out in terror.

And as she sinks into oblivion, the face of one man shimmers in her mind.

The High Priest of the Society of Hermes.

The ancestor of the eminent Lord Langcourt's has murdered the Pythia Cathenna.

And there is nothing Allegra can do about it.

CHAPTER 23

*A*llegra woke up in agony, her low moans drawing Max's attention from outside her room.

He came running, barreling into the room, his face twisted in fear. "You're awake," he said, his eyes wide and empty. There were dark circles accenting his pale, almost gray skin, and she realized he must have been worried.

But she couldn't spend any further time thinking about what Max felt because she was more focused on the fierce stabbing pain in her back.

"He stabbed me," she groaned as she moaned, then tried to clutch her back. The location of the pain made it difficult and she realized the killer had been smart.

"What? Who?" Max stared around the room, frantically searching the corners, the window and even spun on his heel to scan the bathroom.

"No . . . not here," she whispered.

She watched the pieces slip into place as Max understood what she meant. But before he could say a word a new voice echoed around the room. "Allegra? You're awake. Oh, thank

Apollo." Celestra breezed into the room, hurrying to Allegra's side as Max rounded the bed to check her back.

Allegra couldn't respond to the other woman, the pain from Cathenna's knife wound still filling her back and chest, and only worsening as Max probed her ribs with his fingers.

"What's wrong?" Celestra's voice held a note of fear as she studied the agonized expression on Allegra's face

Allegra inhaled slowly, and turned to look at Max whose expression was one of stunned confusion. He held out his fingers, showing the stained tips to Allegra.

Despite the pain she wriggled into a seated position and stared at his fingers. "But it was just a dream."

He wiggled his fingers. "Clearly not. We need to get you seen to."

Allegra shook her head.

"If you are bleeding then the wound could be dangerous."

"How much blood?"

Max bent to inspect her back, lifting her night shirt to study what Allegra assumed was a knife wound. He grunted then dropped the hem and sat back.

"That is odd."

"What's odd?" both Allegra and Celestra asked in unison.

"There is no wound. Just blood staining your skin."

"That is weird." Allegra wasn't sure how to deal with that. "Nothing very small, near invisible?"

Max shook his head. "Nothing."

Allegra sat back against the pillows, trying to figure out what had just happened. Celestra stood beside the bed, her confused expression echoing what Allegra was feeling.

Allegra looked up at the other woman, unsmiling. She just couldn't muster the energy to fake a smile. "I'm sorry, Celestra. Things must be a little strange for you."

Celestra shrugged. "It's okay. I expect strange when it comes to people who can see the future." She smiled. "And it's Les."

"Les?" Allegra found herself lost for a moment.

"Call me Les. I've always found Celestra a bit of a mouthful."

Allegra let out a soft laugh. "Sorry. Brain's a little fuzzy right now." She glanced up at Max wondering if she should be mentioning anything in Celestra's—Les's—presence. Max appeared noncommittal, not even giving Allegra the courtesy of a nod.

Annoyed, she shifted to move her feet toward the edge of the bed. When Les gave her a questioning glance, Allegra said, "You're willing to fetch me a bedpan? Or a diaper? I need to pee." She raised an eyebrow.

Les chuckled making Allegra smile. At least Les had a sense of humor. Allegra got to her feet slowly and walked to the bathroom under her own steam.

She'd been terrified to touch . . . Les—she was going to have to get used to the new name. She wasn't ready for another vision. Not right now.

In the bathroom, she stared at her reflection. Although hard to accept, she had to face the fact that her time spent with Cathenna was no vision. It was no dream, or anything summoned by fatigue, stress or drugs.

Allegra reached out and placed her fingers on the mirror. She'd traveled back in time. As unlikely as it sounded, it was true. And she'd experienced Cathenna's death first hand.

And she'd been unable to do anything about it.

Guilt threatened to drown Allegra, to take all the breath from her lungs and leave her with nothing.

She gripped the porcelain of the washbasin, and clenched her eyes shut. There, against the screen of her eyelids she saw the face of Cathenna's killer. A face that looked exactly like Lord Langcourt, High Priest of the Order of Hermes.

Langcourt's ancestor had murdered a Pythia. It was no wonder that Langcourt wished to continue the tradition.

Allegra let out a soft groan; partly from pain, partly from

frustration but mostly from grief. She'd felt an inexplicable affection for Cathenna, a woman she'd connected with over the space of centuries.

That fact made no sense at all, and yet it made total sense to Allegra given that she was still suffering the pain from the deadly wound inflicted upon her by Langcourt's forefather.

She needed to speak to Max about the details, about Thrasius, Cathenna's husband, and about the Pythia's horrible death.

Straightening, Allegra pushed her hair from her face and inhaled deeply, shoving against the pain in her back. She had to get past it. She refused to let it control her, to be debilitated by her reaction to the whole experience.

Come what may she planned to do something about Cathenna's murder. She wasn't sure if Pythias had always been complacent, or if they'd had their own ways to protect against, and investigate such horrific crimes against their order. Having no knowledge or education on the subject, she was going to have to take the matter into her own hands.

Allegra used the washbasin to support her weight as she turned and moved to the door. Inside the room, Max was pacing while Les remade the bed.

Allegra walked to the closet.

"What do you think you are doing?" Max's voice was sharp.

Allegra glanced over her shoulder. "I can't waste time wallowing in misery and injury. There are things I need to do."

"Would you at least rest for a minute? Whatever it is you need to do can surely wait until you have rested a bit. We can get you what you need."

Allegra stopped and turned, taking in Max's haggard expression, the coarse stubble on his chin, Les's disheveled hair and creased dress. The sight of her two rumpled nurses gave Allegra pause.

Surely if they could sacrifice their own time and energy on her, she could at least take a small breath. Cathenna's killer was dead, but his descendant was alive, and while he still drew breath she wasn't about to allow him to get away with his attempt to kill Allegra herself.

With a small nod she returned to the bed and sank onto the mattress.

She lifted her hands as Les drew the covers over her lap. As she relaxed her hands, her forearm bumped into Les's wrist and the room twisted and disappeared.

CHAPTER 24

*W*hen Allegra opened her eyes she'd expected to see the hovel in which she'd first found Les's body. Instead she found herself staring at a red-and-creme marble floor where a drop of dark red blood glistened in the pale moonlight streaming into the room through a trio of floor-to-ceiling windows.

Pale curtains billowed inward, color stripped in the light of the moon. A frigid breeze invaded the room, bringing with it a chill enough to turn Allegra's bones to ice.

Outside, the sky was heavy with dark clouds swollen with rain. The clouds clustered together leaving oddly shaped gaps through which the fragmented moonlight shone so brightly it hurt to look at.

Allegra straightened and focused on the floor before her again, her attention on the glistening drop of blood. Slightly oval in shape it had a tiny outward point to one edge, indicating its owner had been moving in the direction of a room across the living area in front of Allegra.

Allegra wanted to look away but she knew if she didn't commit it all to memory she wouldn't remember.

Without realizing it she began to describe everything around her out loud, hoping it would remain in her memory long enough for her to remember when she came back to consciousness.

She followed in the wake of the droplets, hoping they would lead her to something that made sense. Through the room Allegra moved, studying the marble floors and the trail of droplets as it led her all the way to the bathroom.

At the threshold Allegra paused, her foot almost flattening a little blue stuffed bear. Its beady little pink eyes stared back at her but she barely paid it any attention.

She was focused on finding Les—because she'd assumed this would be a vision of Celestra's future considering the other woman had been the one to touch Allegra's bare skin.

But everything was different and Allegra had a strong suspicion that the dream was something else. Could it be a vision like the one she'd had of Cathenna, traveling all the way back two thousand years?

Allegra studied the room, comfortable that everything was as modern as it ought to be.

She shook her head sharply—or perhaps she only imagined doing it—and focused on the empty room.

The clouds had shifted, and a blanket of darkness had fallen almost instantly upon the room, but Allegra's eyes didn't require adjusting to the change in the light.

On the marble tiles of the bathroom floor ran a trail of droplets, leading Allegra through and into the bedroom beyond.

Allegra came to a sudden halt, her legs turning to stone, refusing to move any closer.

Here too the windows had been flung wide open, the curtains gusting, billowing inside, almost obscuring the woman who lay half inside and half on the balcony.

She lay deathly still, her white satin gown spread out almost as if she was in flight. One arm lay on the floor beside her head, so innocently, as if she lay there asleep, resting inches from her face, fingers curled and half opened.

The other hand lay at her side, a long shard of glass within her grip. Blood coated her fingers, her tight grip having bitten down so hard on the jagged shards, drawing blood enough to coat the tiles beneath her hand.

Allegra forced her body to move, forced her consciousness to live this vision through. It was only a vision. Only a glimpse into the future.

It's not real.

Allegra shifted closer to the body, angling just so, hoping to identify the woman as someone other than Les. Had she not know the woman so well, not spent so much time with her in the last few days, she could have easily not recognized her.

But she did know her.

Despite the swollen flesh around both her eyes, the bloody broken skin on her cheekbones and the torn lips.

Les lay dead on the floor at Allegra's feet.

Her head lay at an odd angle and one more step to Allegra's right and her eyes widened. Celestra's neck was a gaping, bloody mess. Someone had slit her throat open, the amount of blood—now obsidian stains in the light of a heartless moon—confirming it as the death blow.

They'd beaten her within an inch of her life, and then slit her throat.

This wasn't supposed to have happened. They'd warned Les, she'd listened, agreed to go back to the States. So why was she still dead in the future?

Allegra took a breath and found her vision fading. Just before she closed her eyes her fading gaze fell on a small object lying beside Celestra's bloodied hand.

A small pink blue-eyed toy bear drenched in blood.

CHAPTER 25

*A*llegra blinked, regaining her senses as the room came into focus. Her heart raced, only slowing when she recognized her room at the embassy. She pushed herself to sit up and stared around her, her attention focusing first on Max and then the shadow of Les's form in her peripheral vision.

She tilted her chin to meet Max's gaze and he moved to sit at her side, setting a writing pad and pencil onto the mattress beside him. His spine was rigid, his features tight and dark.

"How do you feel?" he asked, his voice a rumbling baritone, far deeper than his normal speaking voice.

Allegra frowned. "What's the matter? Did something happen while I was asleep?"

He shook his head and shifted closer, placing his hand on her forehead. She swatted his fingers away. "I'm not sick, Max."

"I don't expect you to be. I just want to be sure, okay. So relax." His tone was firm, a little too sharp if you asked Allegra. Scowling she submitted while he checked her temperature, the blood vessels in her eyes and her heart rate.

When had he suddenly taken such interest in her medical well being?

When you were almost shot to death? a voice murmured in her head.

Even the voice in her head was acting odd.

Allegra waited until Max sat back. "So? Am I cleared? Will I live?"

Max nodded, ignoring her attempt at lightening the mood. Instead he looked over at Les still standing just inside the door. Her skin was pale, and she looked like she'd just seen a ghost.

"Could you give us a minute?" he asked softly.

Les hesitated, her gaze going from Max's face to Allegra's. She stared for a moment at Allegra, her expression confused, her mouth opening as if to ask a question.

But Max cut her off. "Les? Please?" He got to his feet and walked over to the other woman. His ex. Allegra had to keep reminding herself of that fact. Why did it not rip her apart with jealousy? Oh maybe because she and Max were not in a relationship so she didn't have a say in who he saw, or what he did in his personal life.

She shook the thoughts off and Max returned to sit beside her.

"What is it? You look like I took a sledgehammer to your skull."

He snorted. "I'd say that's just about what you did."

Allegra frowned, more confused than ever. Then she thrust the thoughts from her head. "Look. I can't get distracted or waste any time, Max. I have to relay what I saw before I forget the details." She shifted to the side of the bed, pausing when the room began to spin a little too fast.

Max put a hand on her shoulder. "Stop. Just sit there for a few more minutes. You can't just go rushing off. You're not even healed from the bullet wound. You had no business going into a vision now of all times."

Allegra snorted. "Oh? That's because I know exactly how to summon the damned things, huh?"

Max began to pace. "I'm sorry. I didn't mean that. It's just that things have gone a little off the plot."

"At least you had a plot," muttered Allegra as she scooted up the bed to lean against the pillows. "I'm still wondering if such a thing as a plot exists in my strange life." She was musing, and so hadn't expected Max to respond.

"You'll have to forgive me. I've been a little unfair to you," he said, startling her.

She watched him warily, unsure if she really wanted to hear this terribly ominous revelation.

"The vision you just had—"

Allegra gasped, reminded that the details of that vision were slowly disintegrating. "Max, I have to tell you everything."

He looked up at her and simply said, "You've already told me."

"What?" Allegra said, her voice so soft she may as well have whispered.

Max nodded. He leaned across Allegra's knees and picked up the pad and pencil. Without a word, he handed it to her and got to his feet to pace as she flipped through the pages.

His script was long and dramatic, giving the contents an even deeper resonance. Or perhaps that came from Allegra having experienced it firsthand.

Or was it secondhand given that it was a vision?

She focused on the words, seeing Max had taken down almost everything she'd said, with only a few blank spaces; likely moments when she'd been speaking too fast for him to keep up.

As Allegra stared at the words, a thought made her stiffen. She'd spoken the words of the vision out loud.

She looked up sharply. Although his back was to her he seemed to sense her attention, and pivoted on his heel to meet her eyes. Allegra's stare penetrated Max's hooded gaze, even as her heart sank.

"Celestra was in the room?"

Max nodded. "She heard every word you said."

CHAPTER 26

The silence in the room hung between them, heavy and almost tangible. Max shifted, his hands searching his waist for a place to hide, for something to do that would mask the tension in his muscles, the tight grip of his fists.

He nodded and sank onto the bed. "It was too late. You scared us, and Les . . . she didn't want to be anywhere else."

"You should have known better," said Allegra, her tone hard and cutting. "We cannot allow her to get too involved in our mission. You of all people should know that."

He nodded and rested his elbows on his thighs to support his head in his open palms. "I wish I could change what happened. But you were so . . ." He shook his head and straightened, twisting in position to face her. "There isn't time beat around the bush. What happened today was dangerous. Nobody, and I mean nobody, can know." He gave her a harsh look.

Allegra shook her head, not sure what she was supposed to take from that. "You mean because I spoke my vision out loud?"

Max took a breath and got to his feet. "The last time a Pythia spoke her dreams without assistance, dreams not attributed to Apollo, she was crucified, then burned alive. Roman rule at the time didn't suffer witchcraft, nor did they parse too much of a difference between seer's visions and demonic worship."

"So, you're afraid that if people found out I voiced my visions without the need of an interpreter—" Allegra stiffened. "Wait one moment." She lifted her hand, waving it in the air to stop Max as he opened his mouth to speak.

"I needed to tell you something else. Another vision that I had of Cathenna."

"When?" Max stared at her in confusion and then, his expression cleared. "The stabbing."

Allegra gave a half nod. "We haven't had much of an opportunity to talk." Then she let out a soft laugh. "It was such a strange, confusing vision, and in the end such a terrible one that I think I may have needed time to absorb it."

"You certainly did absorb it with that stab wound."

"It wasn't really a wound. More like a phantom memory of what Cathenna had experienced." Allegra took a shaky breath. "But it's probably best that I explain it to you."

Max nodded then glanced at the door.

And Allegra said, "But it can wait until after we talk to Les. She needs some comfort and it's probably best she isn't left alone for too long. Not right now."

"You think she's in danger even within the embassy?"

"Maybe. But it's not the external dangers I'm worried about. We need to know what she is thinking. For her own safety."

Max nodded and headed to the door. He opened it and poked his head out into the living area. A moment later he stood aside to let Les in. She entered bearing a tray of iced teas and light snacks—mainly cheeses, cut fruit and breads. She set the tray on the bed and sat beside Allegra, her expression somber.

"You need your strength if you want to get better faster." Without looking at Allegra she prepared a plate, handing it over with a serviette. The last thing Allegra wanted to do was eat, but the tremor in Les's hands as she passed the food had forced

Allegra to remember that there was more to this picture than just her own emotional turmoil.

She ate while Max fiddled with the papers and picked at the cheese and grapes on his own plate.

A few minutes later, Allegra said, "So you heard it all?"

Les shrugged a single shoulder. "I should have known to be more careful and not touch you." Her voice was dull, as if she was too tired to care.

Allegra leaned forward. "Regrets are only regrets because they are too late." She shook her head, the movement drawing Les's gaze. "It was so different. Things changed this time. The vision itself had changed in so many ways and yet, the outcome was the same."

Les's face was pale as her gaze drifted to Max, seeking reassurance in his eyes. She didn't find it. Max's attention was focused on the sheaf of papers in his hand.

Allegra touched Les's arm and when the woman flinched, Allegra said, "Don't worry. I suspect I won't see anything more at least for a day or two." Then she paused, still holding Les's gaze. "I need you to be totally honest with me, Les. Have you been entirely truthful with me?"

Les paled, her gaze shifting away from Allegra's for the briefest moment. "I am. I promise. I've told you all I know."

Despite Les's words, Allegra had a strange sense that the woman was lying.

With a shake of her head Allegra sat back, her spine stiff as she searched her memories. And unexpectedly, they came rushing back in such a wave of images and emotions that tears flooded her eyes and she had to blink rapidly to hide them.

Her vision shifted and the memories of the apartment were overlaid upon her room. She saw Celestra's bloodied corpse like a movie projected upon the image of the doomed woman, still alive and well, her eyes lined and her shoulders bowed.

"The apartment?" Allegra said, her words making Les flinch. "Do you know the place?"

Les shook her head, staring at Allegra in confusion. Max cleared his throat. "Some of it I missed. And at some point your words were ... garbled."

Allegra nodded, feeling her heart filling with dread. She'd hoped she'd have the easy way out, but now she was forced to repeat what she'd seen, give voice to Celestra's horrific death, hear her own word falling like jagged spikes filled with fear.

Max's gaze said she really had no choice. And so she inhaled slowly and described the room, the pale tiles, the billowing curtains and the view of a dark and terrible sky.

Through the transparent vision of the room, Allegra could see Les's pale, shocked face as she described the blood trail and the bedroom filled with shadows and death.

She finished her retelling, keeping one crucial detail to herself. The time wasn't yet right and she wanted to hear more from Les first.

When the room was silent and all she could hear was Les's ragged breathing and the scraping of Max's pencil on his pad of paper, Allegra leaned forward.

Les had been staring out the window at the view of the gigantic Pyramid of the Emperor, and Allegra's movement drew her gaze. There was a blank, emotionless quality within their depths that made Allegra's heart clench.

Allegra swallowed and said, "Do you know the apartment, Les?"

Celestra couldn't evade Allegra's gaze, nor could she avoid answering the question. She gave a sharp nod. "It's my apartment back at the Capital." Fear flitted across her face and her expression faded to ice. "Why did you have to do this to me?" she asked, her tone rising as she got to her feet and glared at Allegra.

Max stirred, glancing up from his writing. "Les?" he said, a note of warning in his tone.

"Don't Les me. You know what she did. Why did she have to come here and put me in this position? If she'd just left everything alone, just stayed out of everyone's business, these stupid visions of hers wouldn't come true." Les snapped her gaze to Allegra, her eyes now hard and angry. "What they say about you is true. You're nothing but an interfering bitch, pushing her way into things that don't concern her."

Allegra's jaw dropped. She'd expected a dramatic reaction, but not one filled with hysteria and paranoia. She glanced helplessly at Max, and was disappointed to see her worries reflected in his eyes.

He got to his feet as Les continued, "If you know what's good for both of you you'll take her and leave this place. Before you cause more innocent people to be killed."

Max reached out and put his arms around her, and then she began to cry, pushing Max away and swiping the heel of her hand across the stream of tears on her cheeks. "Get out of here, go!" She screamed the words, and Max grabbed her by the shoulders giving her a solid shake.

"Les," he said, keeping his tone even and calm.

Whether it was his voice, or the mention of her name, Les fell silent, her body shuddering as if in shock. Her words came out in a whisper. "Dear Hera . . . the bear."

Something was very, very wrong here and Allegra meant to find out what it was. But one thing was clear.

Now was not the time.

Allegra wasn't entirely sure what Les was talking about, or what bear she referred to. For a moment she stilled, as if something at the edge of her memory was waving out to be heard, but try as she might she couldn't quite grasp hold of it.

Allegra knew she'd missed something crucial but she couldn't put a finger on it.

For now, she would have to put it at the back of her mind and deal with the problem at hand.

"Allegra?" Max's voice broke through her worries.

"Sorry . . . what?" she asked, distracted.

"Can you try to recall anything that would help us pinpoint a time? Anything you can remember just to be sure it's not in the immediate future?"

Allegra nodded and sank into the memory again, going through it frame by frame to pick it all apart.

She shook her head. "Maybe the moon? But that's hard because you'd have many options and you'd likely be able to pin a time of the month on it from the fullness of the moon, but you'd have an opportunity once a month for Apollo knows how many years."

Max was silent, and Les shrugged his arm away, giving him an apologetic look. He didn't seem to notice either the rejection or the regret. "She still dies."

Allegra nodded even though it hadn't been a question.

"What can we do?"

"I don't know." Allegra sighed, her shoulders bowed now as her strength began to fade.

"We have to get her out of Qusqu. Fast."

Allegra shook her head. "You'll likely just send her to her death. We avoided her death here, but the very fact that this vision shows her death now taking place in her home in the Capital means we didn't save her. We just postponed her death."

"Then what do we do?"

"What we can't do is put Les in danger." Allegra nodded. She had a plan and she hoped Max would agree. She wasn't sure how he'd feel, considering her choice of destination, but it was as good a plan as she could come up with on the spot.

She looked up at Max who suddenly appeared to have aged decades.

"We take Celestra away with us."

CHAPTER 27

"What do you mean the Pythia was shot?" Langcourt shook with fury. "What did you do?" he spat, glaring at Roquefort who stood behind him with a stiff spine.

"I assure you, sire, I did nothing to instigate such an act." The man's voice quavered and Langcourt felt only slightly comforted that he would not have been responsible.

"Then will you find out who is behind it?" Langcourt stabbed a finger onto the desk, pressing so hard that his joints bent at a dangerous angle. "I want the woman dead, but it must be by my own hand. Nobody, and I mean nobody, is allowed to kill her besides me. I want her brought to me alive. Do you hear me? Alive."

Roquefort nodded, then scurried out of the room, leaving Langcourt still vibrating with anger. He took his finger off the table, feeling the slight twinge in the joint from the pressure. He massaged the bones and glared at the stone-walled room. He felt impotent, unable to do anything without someone else doing it for him. He hated being so removed from the agents who were doing his bidding. Hated not being in total control of the local priests and their cults.

The room was bright, filled with light, the late afternoon sunshine giving the gray stone a golden glow. Still, he longed for home, even if it meant dull and dreary Londinium skies.

He'd given his instructions to Roquefort, to make the arrangements to capture Allegra Damascus. Though the last time he'd wanted her in his custody, it had been for the sole purpose of sacrifice. He'd been determined to do just that, despite the disagreement of his brothers in the Society of Hermes.

In the end, she'd escaped. Someone had aided her, but Langcourt had no way of knowing who. Especially not since his entire estate had been blown to smithereens.

Perhaps that had been a tad of an overreaction, but he had managed to kill a good number of the Brittanic policemen who had raided his home.

After Allegra had escaped she must have reported her abduction to the police, but Langcourt had been certain she'd had no way of knowing who he was, or where she'd been held captive.

So he suspected it had been an inside job.

Not Roquefort, of course. The man wasn't bright enough to plot behind Langcourt's back that way.

Still, Langcourt supposed that, given the Pythia was still alive, he still had his chance to capture her for his own requirements. He just had to be smarter and faster.

Langcourt still had one ace up his sleeve.

His mole at FAPA was still feeding him good intelligence.

And what he'd last heard had made him want to rail at the gods at the injustice of it all. Again he was thwarted by one of the Oracle's prophecies. From the word going around at FAPA, Allegra was in Qusqu investigating a prophecy which had something to do with major citywide destruction. His contact knew no more than that.

Which was understandable, yet supremely frustrating.

Langcourt had had little contact with the rest of the elite from Hermes, but word—from those who were still his men to command—was everyone had agreed it was in the best interest of the whole Society that the Pythia be left alone. They were still strongly convinced that Allegra was important to the world.

Langcourt disagreed.

The other members were cowards, afraid of their own tails, afraid to take danger by the horns, afraid to endanger their standing in the community, within society.

Hidden in a room beneath his estate, they'd been men who'd appeared brave, determined, courageous. But now, given the opportunity to act upon those same principles, they backed away like cowards. Langcourt had to wonder if some of those very men had turned on him, had redirected their loyalties, as the rich elite found it all so easy to do.

And so now he was at an impasse with them. They'd decreed that the Pythia will live. But Langcourt had never been the type of man to bow to another man's rules. He'd do what he wanted. Especially when it came to the Pythia.

He had history with her and her lineage going back two entire millennia.

Memories surged up within his mind and he lashed out, slamming his fist into the side of a five-foot-tall urn, one of two flanking the window.

His knuckles smarted, skin splitting leaving a sharp trail of blood on the colorless stone. The urn wobbled on its base then tilted over. Langourt remained motionless as the urn began to tilt away from him, falling hard onto the ground, and shattering into hundreds of pieces.

His hand hurt but he would never admit it. Not to himself and more importantly not to anyone else.

He had a reputation to uphold. He'd never tell anyone of his failures.

Failure is weakness.

He took a deep breath and turned to stare at the giant book on his desk. Roquefort was slowly expanding the genealogy of the Pythias and Langcourt had to now find a way to slip in information the man could obviously never come by.

Langcourt went to a trunk beside the window. He'd escaped before the fire, taking with him a small number of important items. One of them being his extended research on the oracles and their descendants. He'd made it his life's work to track them all, to know where they were and if ever their power came to fruition.

He withdrew a fat leather-bound envelope and slid out a sheaf of yellowed papers. Taking a few, he inserted them into the pile sitting beside the book the genealogist was working on.

Roquefort would never know.

And all Langcourt needed to do was to remember to retrieve them from the pile before the man stored them away.

Straightening, he left the room, taking care to close and lock the door. Although he'd been given the run of the building by the high priest, Langcourt wasn't about to hand out his trust to anyone, no matter how highly connected they were.

He headed down a long corridor and came to a large open space. It was dank and moldy, covered in moss and littered with dead roaches and the remains of small birds. Feathered corpses lay scattered on the floor, grayed and macabre, tiny rib cages exposed, reaching from within the swollen torsos like miniature fingers begging for mercy.

A fluttering from the high reaches of the room's ceiling drew Langcourt's gaze and he glared up into the shadows in disgust. Bats. He hated the creatures. The breed haunting the pyramid was particularly macabre; a bloodsucking creature that hunted out warm-blooded animals to partake of a meal of fresh blood. True fodder from which awful legends were born.

Langcourt took a path along the edges of the room, studying the items hanging upon rusted nails driven deep into the stone. Masks of desiccated leather, some in such terrible repair they were almost falling apart, hung five to six feet apart, all staring out into the middle of the room as if eternally watching one single space.

The direction of their gazes all collided at one single point. A square stone altar, only a hands-breadth wide sat like a lonely monolith. Even from where he stood twenty feet away, Langcourt could make out the chips and scrapes created by a blade slamming into stone. He could imagine the sacrificial victim— willing or unwilling would not have mattered, of course—lying prone, awaiting the fall of the blade.

Langcourt smiled.

A much more hands-on method than the guillotines he'd seen come out of Frankia during the revolution against Roman rule.

Langcourt found it fascinating, this room filled with its terrible secrets, of death and sacrifice, of blood spilled, of the cries of the innocent.

And all while the death faces of twenty men stood watch.

CHAPTER 28

*M*ax arranged a car for Celestra, which made Max wonder what type of service it was that would take her to her squatter-town hovel.

As soon as he put the phone down, Allegra asked him as much.

His response was a shrug. "Maybe that's not really her home. Maybe it is, and McIvor doesn't know?"

"Maybe it's a bad idea to send her back there?" said Allegra. She was still pale from her gunshot wound, and then the strange stab wound she'd awakened with.

Max paused and beyond Allegra's shoulder he saw Les's spine stiffen. He frowned, still considering Allegra's comment. "You could be right." He shifted to the right to meet Les's eyes. "Anything at home that you need?"

She shook her head, the bleakness in her gaze making his heart twist. He wished he could help her but there was a wall between them now, a wall defined by the hurt of the past.

Max shifted on his feet. "I think you should stay here." When she didn't respond he asked, "Do you have family or friends we should notify?"

Les looked up and met his gaze. "Not if I want to keep them safe."

A chill trickled down Max's spine, something in those words making him feel like he'd missed something.

Max nodded. "Probably for the best. I'll arrange for an extra bed to be brought up."

Les got to her feet and smoothed down the front of her skirt. "And who do you think you will be contacting to make such arrangements for you?" There was a small tilt to the corner of her lips as she spoke and she rolled her shoulders back and took a deep breath. "It's probably time I gave the impression I actually work here."

She headed for the door then stopped and turned to looked at Allegra. "I hope you know—"

Allegra held up a hand. "I understand. There is no need for an apology."

Les's eyes glistened as she nodded and headed for the door. The door clicked shut behind her and Allegra turned to face Max. "It's way past time to tell you about Delphi."

Max nodded and took her elbow, leading her to a sofa near the window. A cool breeze soughed through the open windows and Allegra sighed.

"That first dream . . . I said I wasn't sure what it was, if it was just a vision, or a dream. But this time I think it's much more than a vision. I think I saw into the past. Or if not, then perhaps it's a residual memory handed down through the generations of Pythias."

"Perhaps," Max murmured. "And perhaps you need to tell me what you saw?"

Allegra smiled weakly and proceeded to outline her vision, following her awakening within Cathenna's drug-induced haze, to the sense of her affection for her translator.

At the mention of the translator Max's gut had tightened. There was so much he had to tell Allegra, but her visions were giving her that information without the need for his intervention.

All well and good, but would Allegra understand his omissions?

He steeled his emotions as she continued, detailing her recognition of the gathering of senators including the Langcourt-doppelganger, and lastly the realization that Thrasius and Cathenna had in fact been married. With children.

Max's stunned expression only reflected Allegra's own reaction to the vision.

But there was an almost tangible horror in his heart, one he was certain reflected clearly upon his face as she described the murder of the Pythia Cathenna, and the identity of her killer.

He listened to Allegra voice the truth behind who Max himself was and found it hurt deeply that he'd never been able to bring himself to tell her the truth.

He'd lain the blame at Aurelia's feet. She'd cautioned him against being hasty, tried her best to convince him that whatever his emotions told him, he'd need to be patient more than anything.

Her belief was oracles, whether Pythia or seers, were not immune to the darkness. "Even oracles can be bad people," she'd said in her matter-of-fact tone. "You would have to be certain you can trust her. And not just certain. You will need to know beyond a shadow of a doubt that she was true to her destiny, true to her bloodline."

Max had countered with the wisdom of an eighteen-year-old boy. "What if I don't care for her?"

Aurelia had laughed. "My boy, I'm afraid it does not work that way." She hadn't elaborated, and had just sat there smiling at him, her rheumy eyes glistening in the sun. At the time he'd wondered what she meant, had questioned her assertion that he had no choice.

How could he have no choice of his own fate?

Max wanted to laugh at the memory of the naive boy he'd once been.

Choice had been something to hold tight to his heart, to revel in the possession of it as if it were a sword to wield against the world itself.

How little had he known of what fate had in store?

Choice had played no role in his pursuit of Aurelia's successor, in his persistence of tracking the charlatan seer of Las Suertes. He'd been hell bent on proving to Aurelia that she was wrong.

He'd believed he had. Until the day he'd met Allegra on the beach below her home.

Emotion had flooded him. Admiration for her spirit and her independence. Amusement at how alike she was to Aurelia, her wit and her sharp tongue.

Shock when Xales had appeared and had almost impaled Max.

Joy when Max had confirmed who Allegra was.

And just now she'd spoken Thrasius' name as if his existence was entirely acceptable. But Max had to remind himself that Allegra would have had no way to know that Thrasius and Cathenna would have been destined to be a mated pair. That fate and the stars, that destiny and tradition had conspired to bring them together.

Max knew his face had revealed his shock but Allegra seemed not to have noticed, seemed so engrossed in her retelling that she barely registered his reaction.

Thrasius, the fated father. Aurelia has spoken of him, used him as an example of the total, devoted loyalty of the Immunis to his Pythia. Could Max be as devoted to Allegra as his predecessor had been?

And the fate that had befallen Cathenna and her mate weighed heavily on Max. He shook his head. Had he grown so weak in his time away from FAPA duty that the persecution and murder of two people who'd died almost two millennia ago could affect him so all-encompassingly?

He'd been so deep within his thoughts that it took him a while to realize Allegra was waiting for him to respond to something she'd said. She regarded him with a suspicious look, and he shifted his gaze. He was all too aware that Allegra knew him well enough to tell he was lying to her about something

She stared at him and he turned away, looking out at the view of the city.

When the silence fell, Max's thoughts went back to Langcourt's doppelgänger. Was there some connection between Langcourt and his murderous forefather? Both the men certainly seemed to have borne a hatred for Pythias. A fact that made Langcourt a potential threat to Allegra's life.

And one that could verify that Langcourt was digging deeper into Allegra's origins. A truth Max was not about to allow Langcourt to get his hands on.

That was a secret Aurelia had insisted be revealed to Allegra and Allegra alone.

Max turned to meet Allegra's gaze. "We need to prepare to leave as soon as possible."

"I'm just a little worried about leaving Qusqu without finding out more about the killings and the destruction of the city." Allegra's face was shadowed and Max could see her fatigue in the dark hollows beneath her eyes.

"I understand but you can't keep getting visions while you are this weak. You're still relatively new to seeing, and the traveling to the past—or whatever that was—is taking its toll on you. A dead Pythia sees no visions."

Allegra let out a short laugh, her eyes sparkling for a moment. "You think you're funny?"

"I know I am." He headed over to her and helped her to her feet, the action reminding himself of his attendance to Aurelia in her frailer times. "I'm taking you to bed so come quietly. Or I *will* carry you."

Allegra merely grunted while Max felt his head heat up as he registered his words.

He'd very much like to take Allegra to bed, but the time and the place seemed out of reach. He was beginning to wonder if he'd ever get to opportunity to make up for the Aulus debacle.

As he drew Allegra back to the room and waited as she climbed in, Max's mind was leaning toward things far less sedate than putting Allegra to bed. He imagined bare legs entangled with the sheets, glistening with sweat in the aftermath of love-making in the heat of the day.

Max swallowed and shoved the thoughts out of his head as he drew the covers over Allegra's leg.

"Now get—" The doorbell chimed and Max gritted his teeth. "Now who can that be?"

Allegra didn't respond, her eyelashes fluttering as her lids began to close. Exhausted was a good description.

He left her and hurried to answer the door, more than surprised to see the ambassador's wife giving him a worried smile.

"Hello, Commander," she said as she sailed into the apartment. She looked around, then faced Max. "How is the Pythia feeling? I must apologize for not coming to see her earlier. I'm afraid I was detained unexpectedly."

"We understand, Elana. It's no matter. The Pythia has been resting."

"Ah yes, she does need her rest. I'm glad Celestra has been in attendance."

Max nodded. "Yes. She's been most helpful. I'm not sure we could manage without her."

Elana nodded and Max said, "I'll see if she is awake." He hurried back inside the room to check on Allegra who now appeared to be half awake. Still he didn't want to disturb her, especially not now when it looked like exhaustion was building up for her.

He turned on his heel to inform Elana that the Pythia was not taking visitors only to see the ambassador's wife had entered the room two feet behind him. She ignored Max and sailed to the side of the bed.

"Oh, my Lady. You do look dreadful," she said, her tone sharp as she met Max's eyes. "Have you been taking care of her? The doctor did say she needed rest."

Max was at first taken aback at her question, but then was focused on her comment regarding the doctor. Had the ambassador asked the doctor to report in on Allegra's condition?

Max bristled. So much for doctor-patient-confidentiality.

"Elana, I assure you they've been taking very good care of me," Allegra said softly. There was a tiny hint of irritation in her tone but Max couldn't tell if it was due to being disturbed when she was almost asleep, or if she'd registered the criticism in the woman's voice and words.

"I'm so glad of it," Elana said, reaching out to pat Allegra's hand.

Before Max could stop her, Elana's bare skin made full contact with Allegra's hand.

Allegra flinched and Max knew she was gone.

CHAPTER 29

Drifting to sleep, Allegra felt encased within a warm ball of comfort. Voices in the distance tried to penetrate the fog of her sleep but she wanted to avoid it.

She'd almost succeeded when she felt someone touch her hand.

She flinched but it was too late.

The lethargy of impending sleep disappeared and Allegra was thrust into a room filled with darkness and a wet cold that penetrated to her bones.

She tried to look around her but saw nothing but darkness. As her gaze flitted left and right she caught flashes of images but was unable to focus.

Disoriented for a bit, it took a few seconds for Allegra to realize she was encased within some sort of mask. Light entered the darkness in two eye-slits and Allegra concentrated on looking through them, hoping to understand where she was. Or rather, where Elana McIvor was.

This was a vision of Elana's future after all.

One that did not bode well considering she was being held captive, blinded by a hood, unable to move.

Allegra concentrated on the eye-holes focusing on the scene beyond the hood. And her blood ran cold.

She caught flashes of images, people walking back and forth, tall men and women in headdresses, chests bared and oiled. Firelight flickered beyond what Allegra was able to see, the light dancing and reflecting against long iron-tipped spears.

Allegra gasped.

The spears struck a chord within her because she recognized them instantly. The same ancient, hand-carved metal spear-heads that had pierced right through ambassador McIvor's skull.

Her assumption was only verified as she caught sight of McIvor, kneeling on the floor, hands bound, eyes wide as she stared around in shock and terror.

Allegra stilled as she realized where she—or Elana—was. At the scene of the ambassador's murder.

McIvor shuddered, the fear drawing a sheen of perspiration to his forehead. "Wait," he yelled. "You can't do this to me."

"Of course we can. You swore your loyalty. You promised your life in payment for any form of betrayal."

"I didn't betray anyone. I'm loyal. I swear. I am. I'm loyal," McIvor sputtered as his voice rose and then cracked. His terror was clear, almost tangible.

He met Elana's gaze and shook his head. "Why?" he yelled out, pain filling his voice. "Why are you doing this to me?" he asked.

There was an odd note of grief in his voice that made Allegra pause, but she brushed it off. He looked like he was traumatized and she assumed he knew what was coming.

Allegra felt sick to her stomach. *She* knew exactly what was coming for him and she was glad he didn't know.

Allegra gazed at the scene out of Elana's eyes filled with pity for the woman. Held captive and forced to watch her husband's murder, she would likely be traumatized for life.

Not unlike seeing blood on one's hands for months after you're responsible for someone's death.

Allegra shook off the thought and concentrated on the scene in front of her. Beyond the ambassador was a set of stairs leading to a dais of sorts, upon which was a large stone altar. A tall, thin man in a terrifying mask and headdress stood beside the altar, chanting words she did not—and was glad to not —understand.

Allegra's heart thudded against her ribs and she tried to call out. She knew all too well that the nature of the vision was just that; a view to something she really was not a part of. And yet her terror at what was going to happen spurred her to at least try.

The priest on the dais reached into the shadows and withdraw a long staff, tipped with a hand-hewn metal spear, its point so sharp it may as well have been a dagger.

He held the staff forth raising the gleaming tip toward the rays of the moon which entered the room through windows set high above.

Elana was looking at the ceiling and Allegra realized they were within a pyramid. A smaller structure as the ceiling seemed about a hundred feet above them, yet large enough for the highest point to be swathed in darkness.

Windows were scattered along each of the four sides casting crisscrossing patterns of light above their heads. It would have been beautiful had it not been for the horrible circumstances taking place mere meters below it.

The contrast stuck Allegra deeply. Such natural beauty, so pure and untouched, and meters away raw visceral blood gore of murder and sacrifice.

What god would be happy with this?

Allegra took a shuddering breath, aware that Elana was being moved, her footsteps stiff as if resisting her captors and yet afraid for her husband's life.

Was Elana currently under the control of these people? It worried Allegra to think that was the case as it put so much of their plan in jeopardy. If a religious cult was involved with the impending destruction of Qusqu then Max and Allegra were up against so much more than just political machinations.

Cults and gods were not easy to wrestle under control. And neither were the people under their control.

Just how deep McIvor was under this particular cult's control was something Allegra didn't know. He'd seemed familiar enough with them as he'd looked around at his captors. He'd also seemed betrayed enough to know them well.

Perhaps there was a good thing to having this vision.

Beside Allegra light flashed as another priest thrust a spear toward McIvor, the point halting an inch from his right ear. McIvor squealed, the high-pitched sound reverberating within the cavernous ceiling above their heads.

Allegra wanted to yell out at him to grow a pair and stand up for himself, to do something to save his wife from whatever fate was definitely going to befall her.

If these people were to kill him, it would leave Elana at their mercy. Alone.

Allegra moaned and twisted, her eyes opening to her room. Max sat beside her, his face filled with worry. Elana was gone.

Allegra lifted her head off the bed, turned over to rest on her elbow. The room spun but she refused to continue lying down. She needed to do something.

Max was on his feet bedside. "Slow down."

"What happened?"

"Another vision, I assume? You tell me." He quirked an eyebrow as he helped her to sit back upright.

This was becoming a habit she was beginning to dislike.

She glared at him and then scanned the room for Elana. "Is she gone?"

Max nodded. "I think you scared her a little. You passed out and she asked if you were having a vision."

"Hope you told her no."

Max raised an eyebrow. "I did. I said you were very weak and you'd only just gone back to bed when she'd arrived."

Allegra nodded. "Good. The last thing we need is for any of this to get out."

"So, what did you see?"

"Whoever kills McIvor . . . they had his wife. This one happens before he is killed. I saw them inside a pyramid, priest types with religious headdresses and death masks . . . all the chanting and McIvor's cries . . . he was terrified."

"And Elana?" Max asked.

"She was hooded, and bound, I think. I could only see out of two slashes in what felt like a box around my head. It wasn't easy. I was limited solely to where Elana looked in order to see anything at all."

"See any faces?"

She shook her head. "No. The high priest was thin and tall, though."

"You're thinking Qhapaq?"

"Possibly. Or the man with him at the ambassador's ball. Although men that thin and tall are not terribly hard to find here. Have you seen some of the tribal elders?"

Max smiled. "I know. But you haven't yet seen the Emperor. Here he is worshiped as a god merely because he has ancient blood said to have come from the gods themselves."

"No surprise then when people believe so passionately in the priests and their powers."

"Are you thinking that it is likely why you were shot?"

She nodded. "It's possible it was a warning. Or maybe I stirred up embers here a little too much and they need me gone."

"But what could it be? What could they possibly do to cause such widespread destruction to the entire city?"

"That was my next question. In the vision the entire city sank, a gigantic sinkhole for all intents and purposes. What could cause such a thing to occur?"

"Mining?"

"Maybe. Although I doubt it. In these parts mining is frowned upon. And even if it was mining, what is the priests' connection to corporate business dealings."

Max shrugged. "Could be any number of things."

"We could have a crooked priest," murmured Allegra.

"Or a crooked ambassador."

"You were thinking that too?"

Max cracked a grin. "We are on the same wavelength. So yes, it's quite possible. Perhaps he is in league with them. Which would explain Les's involvement."

"It would explain why he kept saying he was loyal. And which would also explain why he'd appeared so shocked at what they were doing to him."

Max got to his feet and began to pace. "I think this means we need to leave here as soon as possible."

Allegra nodded. "I agree. If McIvor is in on it—which is what it appears to be—then Les will continue to be in danger and so will we."

The door opened and Celestra walked in, a shy smile on her face as she set eyes on Allegra.

"Aren't you supposed to be—"

A loud explosion rocked the apartment, throwing Les inside the bedroom. She sprawled on the floor, letting out a stunned moan.

Both Max and Allegra had been shielded by the wall, but from the sounds of glass crashing to the floor, the front of the apartment hadn't been so lucky.

Max rushed to Les, pulling her away from the open doorway. The door which now hung at an angle was tethered to the jamb only by the bottom hinge.

Max dropped Les onto the bed and Allegra helped settle her, checking for injuries.

"Dear Apollo. I think she's just in shock. No injuries that I can see."

Max peered slowly out of the door, cautiously checking the front of the apartment which Allegra imagined was in ruins. "I think it's safe to say that it's time we got out of Qusqu."

Allegra nodded as Max turned to meet her eyes.

"I know you feel things are unfinished here, but I'll get my intelligence people on the case. They're likely to come up with more than what you or I can, especially considering we're so high-profile now."

Allegra nodded. She couldn't disagree. All she knew was it felt like they were running away. At last she took a deep breath and looked up at Max.

"We can leave. But we're going to come back. And when we do, I'm going to make sure nothing bad happens to the people of Qusqu."

CHAPTER 30

*T*hey left Qusqu using the mayhem of the explosion as cover. Celestra had proved resourceful, leading them out of the embassy building through a set of secret tunnels she'd claimed had been built in case an emergency exit was required for the ambassador's and his staff's safety.

The fire engines had roared through the city and the police had raced to the embassy. People milled around the streets across from the building and as Allegra and Max slipped away she felt a sense of horror at the sight of the dark, scorch-marked gash on the side of the front face of the pyramid where their apartment had once been.

Les had suffered a twisted ankle and a burst eardrum. Max and Allegra had escaped with only shock to list as their resulting ailments.

They'd dressed in the hooded cloaks so commonly used by the acolytes of the local tribal cult and though they received some attention, it was more so because of the cloaks than their identities.

Nobody was looking for them yet. For now, they huddled inside a derelict shack overlooking the city. The sun had begun to set and the edges of the horizon had turned a purple-blue. The glow of the fire stood out in stark contrast against the darkening skies.

"Now what?" asked Allegra softly as she huddled with her back against the wall, the city beyond it. The hovel had only half a roof, most of it lying rotten on the floor to their left. She stared at the flickering light reflected against the trees above the building and wondered at where their lives were headed when it was this filled with mayhem.

Max grunted, pulling out his satellite phone. Hopefully whatever help arrived will not be too late as it had been in Indus not too long ago. Corina had died in her arms because of it.

That's not true, said a little voice in her head.

She pushed it away and listened as Max rang his second in command in the States and called in a team to extract them.

When he'd rung off Les asked, "Why didn't they just send a chopper?"

Max pursed his lips. "Because that would draw too much attention. An NGS Army chopper in the air right now would be a dead giveaway that we are escaping."

"Even if the Qusquan law enforcement supports our leaving in such a clandestine way, whoever is after us would be tipped off instantly." Allegra spoke the words without emotion. She was beginning to think too much like Max.

Les nodded and touched her ear gingerly. She winced as her fingers came away stained with blood. "That hurts like a bitch."

Allegra grinned and beckoned her with her hand. "Come, I'll massage it. See if it helps."

Les gave her an odd look.

Allegra laughed softly. "Don't be afraid. I'm a physiotherapist. I know what I'm doing."

Les grinned slightly. "I'm more worried about visions."

Allegra shrugged. "Usually they don't come after I've touched someone once. But I guess if the impending disaster is urgent in any way, or if your relationship to it is relevant, then I'll get the vision of whatever happens no matter who I touch."

Les nodded although she did look skeptical. Still, she shifted closer and allowed Allegra to place her fingers below her ear. The massage wouldn't heal the damage but it would ease some of the throbbing pain she knew came with a burst eardrum.

Hurt like a bitch is exactly the way Allegra would have described it. As her fingers worked she looked over at Max. "How long before extraction?"

He shook his head. "An hour, possibly two. They're sending a team through the jungle so they won't be here fast. We're going to have to hope this hovel will keep us hidden long enough."

Les let out a soft groan which made Allegra smile. Max cracked a grin too. "Ooh, that feels sooo good," Les whispered. Then cleared her throat. "Massages are sometimes even better than sex."

Allegra chuckled. "Best keep that to yourself. Men don't like to hear that kind of thing."

Les laughed. "Well, Max doesn't count."

Before Allegra could ask exactly what she meant by that—because there were two hugely different connotations to her words—a rustling within the tree line made her clamp her mouth shut.

Max lifted a finger to his lips and waved the both of them down. Allegra and Les slid slowly to the floor and waited as Max duck-walked along the far wall toward an open window. After a few minutes in which Allegra's heart thumped so hard she was concerned it would damage her ribs, Max slid back to the ground with a sigh of relief.

"A jaguar," he whispered. "But let's just keep silent in case. And no fire, so I hope we don't end up freezing to death."

Allegra nodded, and so did Les, all thoughts of massages having flown from their heads.

The next hour ticked by. Every so often they checked the view of the embassy building down in the valley. The flames had died down and the milling crowd had only thickened as dense smoke rose into the skies.

The police would have their hands full.

"How long before they start looking for us?" Allegra asked, glancing over at Max who was rifling through his bag. He'd called it a go-bag and had detoured to his bedroom for it before they'd fled.

"Once they clear the apartment and find no bodies. With the damage it could take them a bit, but considering the bedrooms weren't affected they are more likely to assume we escaped to be on the safe side. I know I would."

Allegra nodded. Exhaustion had been building for a while and it was now taking its toll. She blinked away the sleep, but found her head dropping again. She jerked awake so hard that she bumped the back of her head against the stone wall.

"You should sleep. We have a long way ahead of us. I'm guessing a trek through the jungle so both of you should sleep. I'll keep watch."

"What about you?"

Max smiled. "I can manage. And I'm a light sleeper. A few catnaps here and there and I'll be fine."

Though she wasn't too comfortable with leaving him to guard them all by himself, Allegra didn't have much of a choice in the matter. Her eyelids drooped of their own accord and soon she was slipping to the black cocoon of sleep.

CHAPTER 31

The sounds of rustling and low voices woke Allegra and she stared around into the pitch black darkness, her heart racing.

"They're here," whispered Max.

Allegra nodded as she made out his shape across from her. A few other unknown shadows lurked within the shack and she felt a flood of relief. Beside her Les began to stir, and then straighten from leaning against the wall.

"I swear I'm going to get arthritis of the brain if I continue sleeping against this thing. Damn but they're freezing cold."

Allegra grinned. She'd found Les's personality engaging, and so different from the icy, haughty person she'd met on their first day in Qusqu.

Even knowing Les and Max had been together—a long time ago—didn't detract from her growing affection for the other woman.

The extraction team threw a pack in front of each of them, and inside Allegra found full travel gear including thick socks and hiking boots. Considering she'd escaped the apartment wearing a pair of flat sneakers which would never have stood up to a walk through the jungle, Allegra was most appreciative.

Before long the extraction team had them on their feet and following a trail through the jungle. They'd been instructed to step only where the team stepped, and to remain silent unless it was an emergency.

The trek through the jungle took six hours and the sun was on the horizon by the time they reached a small clearing.

One of the men hurried over to Max. "We're out of Qusqu now. Just north of the border. We're waiting on a chopper that'll take you to your location. For your safety, Commander, we won't be asking your destination. You'll be taking the chopper from here yourself, as requested."

Max nodded, scanning the skies looking out for the aircraft. It didn't take long to find it skimming the horizon to the east.

The extraction team, Max, Allegra and Les watched as the chopper closed in on their location, and began to descend.

Allegra's blood ran cold as a low whistling rent the air and the chopper—their only means of escape—burst into flames, sending the watching audience crashing to the ground to take cover.

"What the hell was that?" yelled Allegra above the sound of the roaring of flames consuming the wreckage of the chopper.

The extraction team leader was yelling in Max's ear. When the man was done Max looked over at Allegra.

"That was our pursuers. Whoever they are, they mean business. We need to go into hiding." Max glanced at Les for a moment, an odd expression in his eye. Then he gave her a comforting smile and looked back at Allegra. "Unfortunately, we're going to have to go for a swim.

"Ugh," Les grumbled. "I didn't bring my bathing suit."

Allegra shook her head and smiled as they scrambled to their feet and fled into the trees. Heading north they left the extraction team behind, taking a northeast track into the thickest part of the jungle.

Allegra, though tired, kept pace as best as she could but Les slowed them down, her sprained ankle swelling as they went. They'd stopped three times to rest, during which time Allegra had attended to the sprain, massaging to ease the pain. She couldn't do much more than that, especially since after a good physio session Les would need to rest in order for the joint to begin healing.

Still, Les was a champion, insisting they keep moving, seeming determined not to be the reason they slowed down. The fact that she was too slow was one neither Max nor Allegra voiced out loud.

They were ten minutes from the river when they heard the rushing of the water.

"Be careful of snakes and crocodiles. Oh, and also hippos."

"What?" Les shrieked. "I'm not going into the water with those creatures around."

Allegra shook her head but didn't say anything. It wasn't as if they had much of a choice in how they proceeded. They had everything against them and not even an oracle could help. If she ever learned to hone her skills in order to obtain a vision without the need to touch someone, Allegra knew she would feel more valuable. No longer just a conduit.

They reached a river which amounted to little more than a wide stream rushing over a field of boulders.

Only when they stepped into the water did Allegra realize how deep it was.

Max held his go-bag high above his head while Allegra followed with Les who was also struggling to hold a small pouch up high.

Les let out a squeal as she was sloshed up to her neck. "Max, can you grab this for me. I don't want to get it wet."

Max paused and turned, then reached out for the bag. Les handed it to him and although Allegra was sure he'd managed to grab hold of it, the bag slipped from his grasp and hit the water with a flat smack.

Les screamed and lunged for the bag, but the water swept it away too fast. Frustrated, Les slapped the water and then turned to Max, her gaze furious.

"Sorry, Les. I was sure I had it," said Max, his expression filled with remorse. "I must have been concentrating more on my bag." There was an odd note in his voice and it made Allegra wonder if there was more to his actions than accidentally dropping Les's bag.

Les took a breath and straightened, a little hard to do while almost neck deep in running water but she managed. "It's fine. I suppose I'll have to do without it." She sloshed on, bypassing Max and heading for the opposite bank, fueled by her anger.

As Allegra closed in on Max she asked. "What was that about?"

Max glanced at her but said nothing.

"You dropped her bag deliberately didn't you"

Still not a word.

"Max?"

At last he glanced at her. "Did you wonder how it was we were tracked through the jungle so silently, and how it was they managed to shoot the chopper out of the sky when we had no previous indication they were even here?"

"You think she's transmitting our location,"

"It could only be her." Water sloshed as he took a step closer to the other bank. Les had gotten up onto dry land and was squeezing out her clothing. "I suspect it was a tracker of sorts. Possibly short-range. The long-range ones aren't that trust-worthy yet. Still in the early stages of development."

Allegra looked over her shoulder. "So you think someone is following us, probably close behind?"

Max nodded. "We have to be careful. We're going to change

direction and double back. There's a safe house two hours from here, due south-east."

Allegra nodded. Her blood had grown cold and she wasn't sure which was the stronger contributor; the icy river water or the fact that Les had possibly betrayed them.

Her clothing was sopping wet and clung to her body as she dragged herself up onto the bank. Max tossed his bag up and heaved himself onto the bank, leaning over to give her a hand.

She reached up and grabbed onto his open palm but her hands were wet and muddy and she slipped, bringing him down on top of her.

Max grunted and she looked down to find his face smashed against her boobs.

Allegra began to giggle—while at the same time not unaware of the sizzle of electricity running through her body. Max just lay there, apparently not eager to relocate his body, or his face.

"Move, you big oaf." She shoved at him and he moved away reluctantly. When she got to her feet, she let out an annoyed sigh. "Now I'm all muddy."

She glanced over at the water but Max lifted a hand. "We don't have time. We keep moving. But don't worry. There's a place to bathe at the safe house."

"And how do you know this?"

"Because when I began work with Aurelia, I set up safe stations all across the northern half of this continent. I needed to be sure that whatever happened we'd have various options for safety."

"Very efficient of you," she murmured as she headed up the bank and into the tree line. Les sat on the ground just in front of the tree line emptying water out of her boots.

She looked up at them, and though Allegra expected some comment or quip about their fumble on the water's edge, the other woman said nothing.

Before long they were hiking again, this time heading south-east, Max taking them in a wide arc so Les would not suspect too soon. Not that she'd have any way of alerting the people tracking them unless she built a bonfire, or used gunfire to attract their attention. Neither were a possibility at the pace they were keeping.

Allegra suspected Max was doing it on purpose. To wear Les out and keep her focus on moving rather than coming up with a way to draw attention to their location.

After about three hours of walking Max came to a slow halt, scanning the trees around them. The air was thick with the sound of rushing water and Allegra understood what he'd meant about being able to clean up.

Max led them through the trees, pushing aside a thick clump of trunks growing so close together that they had formed a screen. Slipping between the narrow space they entered a clearing almost entirely hidden by, and covered in trees, leaves and branches. A small hut sat up within the branches of a giant tree. And in the very next tree hung a helicopter, covered in netting and tied to the thick branches by equally thick ropes. A pulley and crank system was set up near ground level, which Allegra suspected would allow them to release and lower the aircraft from its perch within the tree.

Ingenious.

CHAPTER 32

Below the house hung a rope ladder and Max motioned for them to head up. "I'm going to check the chopper. Make sure it's all in order."

Allegra nodded and followed Les who was already halfway up the ladder. The cabin was small but large enough to fit the three of them comfortably.

Large trunks lined the walls, filled with food supplies and drinking water as well as blankets, toilet paper and weapons.

A stack of low camping cots leaned against one wall, which for Allegra was a relief. She hoped—and suspected considering it was broad daylight—they would be waiting for nightfall before they moved off.

Max poked his head through the trapdoor. "If you need to bathe, the waterfall is through the trees over there," he pointed east and Les nodded.

"I call dibs. I need to get out of this wet clothing." She was rifling inside one of the trunks and pulling out dry clothing. Within seconds she was on her feet and hurrying down the ladder, towel wound around her neck, soap and toothpaste hanging from a small net bag.

Allegra and Max watched her walk across the field, and disappear between the trees.

"I hope I'm wrong." Max's voice was hard.

"Don't be angry with her. I have a feeling she's being manipulated beyond our understanding."

"If she doesn't tell us what's going on how can we help her?" Max ran his fingers through his hair, messing up his usually neatly combed mane.

Allegra studied his face. "You still care for her."

It wasn't a question because Allegra could see his turmoil shining in his eyes. She felt a little jolt of fear, a tiny part of her wondering if a relationship had been rekindled within the trauma of the past few days. The only relationship she wanted rekindled was the one between herself and Max.

"Yes. And no." Allegra glanced up, curious. Max cleared his throat. "Yes, I do care for her. She's part of my past, and she's got a place in my heart that won't ever be erased. I used to wish I could wipe it off, like a stain . . . remove it forever to stop being reminded of the end of something special. But now I know I don't need to erase her. What we had was important to the two of us. For a time it worked, but it didn't end well. And now we're here faced with worrying about her distrustful behavior."

A word hung in the air. One he hadn't spoken out loud. *Again.*

"She betrayed you?"

"Not in the normal sense." Max shook his head and bent to sit on a nearby supplies box. "We both knew what we'd wanted out of our relationship, both been aware of each other's purpose. But at some point things changed for her. It became more about *her* needs than mine. And when she gave me an ultimatum—especially one I couldn't acquiesce to—I just couldn't remain in the relationship."

"Partnerships are not about control. I understand why you did it." Allegra spoke softly, watching the light play on his head as the sun's rays shifted through the trees. "I take it she didn't understand?"

Max shook his head. "No, she didn't. It took a few friends explaining to her that she was behaving irrationally for her to stop her insanity."

"And by then it had been too late for you?"

Max nodded. "I couldn't go back to trusting her. I just felt that remaining in a relationship where I was always afraid of the next time she would betray me would put a strain on what I felt for her. I preferred the relationship—not my affection for her —to die."

Allegra nodded and shifted her gaze from his face.

"I know you don't trust me anymore. I'd like to know why." He spoke so softly she almost didn't hear him.

Allegra looked over at Max. "I heard what Aulus said. The instruction he gave you."

Max's eyebrows rose but he didn't appear too surprised. "And you believed I was sent to seduce you. That I obeyed Aulus?"

She nodded.

Max took a breath. "It's true."

Allegra's heart stopped, and she felt a sudden rush of heat filling her head. She almost didn't hear him continue and had to force herself to pay attention.

"I was sent to bring you into the fold. At whatever cost."

Her spine stiffened and she lifted dark angry eyes toward him. He seemed unaffected as a smile grew wide on his face.

"But Aulus always knew I would never sink to such depths. I told him as much. On more than one occasion."

"But he said—"

Max shrugged. "Perhaps he'd hoped you'd overhear and that it would cause friction. Perhaps he merely said it as a reminder to me of what my original orders were. Who knows? Aulus is a manipulative conniving bastard capable of more than you, or I, can imagine. I'd long ago decided never to test him, but I wasn't keen on being controlled especially when it meant I'd have to take advantage of you."

"So . . . does that mean . . ." Allegra wasn't sure what she wanted to say and ended up falling silent as she studied Max's face.

"What it means is you *can* trust me, Allegra. I'm here for you. But there are things I need to tell you. Knowledge that I owe you."

Allegra stiffened. "More things you've kept from me?"

Max smiled. "In a sense, yes. Aurelia forbade me from telling you. She felt you should only know when the time is right. She said I would know when the time is right to tell you, but that I should not rush it."

"Aurelia told you that?"

Max nodded.

"She meant a lot to you . . . Aurelia?"

He nodded again, studying her this time, his expression curious at her line of questioning. "She . . . took me under her wing. She . . . trusted me. And in turn I trusted her, with my life." Max laughed. "I trusted the Pythia Aurelia with the better part of my life. We met when I was fourteen. She was a shrewd old woman and she sought me out, convinced me of my worth and stationed me at her side until her death. She also left me with the responsibility of finding her successor. I swear the woman was one step ahead of me all my life."

Allegra smiled, more at seeing the affection Max had with Aurelia than with the story of his relationship with her. Then she nodded, making the decision in the blink of an eye. "I accept Aurelia's ruling. Whatever it is you need to tell me, you may reveal it when you feel I should know. Until then I will not pressure you, nor will I judge you for waiting."

Max let out a bark of laughter. "You sounded so much like her right now that I'm a little creeped out."

Allegra smiled. "I would have loved to have met her," she said.

"Met who?" asked Les, as she poked her head up into the cabin. Her eyes went from Allegra to Max and back again. "Oh. Aurelia." She fell silent and entered the cabin looking much cleaner and calmer than she had when she'd left.

Max got to his feet and so did Allegra. She dug inside the trunk for clothing and a towel and grabbed the bag of toiletries Les tossed at her. "I'm next. And nobody rush me. I need to wash my hair after the mud-wrestling match with this big oaf."

Max laughed. "Trust me, you won't want to spend too long in there. It may be a little on the cold side this time of year."

"No. It isn't." Les looked over her shoulder. "The falls was actually very warm. Even the water in the pool has steam rising from it."

Max lifted his brows and then said, "Well then. Enjoy your bathing. I need to check out the blades of the chopper so it's ready to go in the morning. Save me some water."

He left the cabin, and Allegra shook her head as she waited for him to jump off the ladder. When she looked up at Les she found the other woman watching her, her expression intense. "You are okay with the whole Aurelia thing?"

"What thing is that?" Allegra asked. The way Les spoke you'd think Max had had an affair with the old woman.

"That he spends so much time with her. Or rather *spent* so much time with her." Les made a face. "I supposed you are the one now . . . who he would be spending that time with . . . so the question would be moot."

Allegra paused. "Was it so bad?" she asked Les.

"What? Sharing him with her?" Allegra nodded. "Only when he was gone. Which felt like all of the time." Les shrugged. "But I was being selfish. I know that now."

"It couldn't have been easy. I can see how that would be hard."

Les shook her head. "No. It was something important to him. But I began to feel like there was no place for me in his life, that she consumed him so much, she left little of him for me. I was selfish, and jealous and I didn't understand. Until now."

"What's different now?"

"You."

"Me?"

"You understand him better than I ever did. It's as if he was made for you and he was just biding his time until you came around."

"That would make him the selfish one."

"No. I don't mean in a conscious sense. I mean . . ."

"I think I understand."

There was an awkward moment in which Allegra wasn't sure what else to say. Then she gave Les a nod and descended the stairs.

CHAPTER 33

*F*ollowing the narrow path through the trees, Allegra made her way in the direction of the sound of crashing water. She came upon the end of the river and stood on the edge, staring down at the cascading water as it fell down into the pool below.

The spray from the falls filled the air, caught by the sunlight and turned into double and triple rainbows that undulated as the misty air moved on the breeze.

Allegra felt the spray coat her skin, surprisingly warmer than she'd expected. As she stared down at the pool she recognized the rising steam, just as Les had described.

Sighing, already feeling the relaxing pull of the warm sunshine, the birdsong and the shimmering rainbows, Allegra picked her way down the narrow path that seemed to have been gouged out the side of the hill.

Her muscles ached now, the trek through the jungle taking its toll on her body. Her calf and thigh muscles burned and she sighed with relief when she finally reached level ground.

The pool was large and from its blue-black color she guessed it was not terribly deep. Steam curled from the surface and lay over the water like a pale ghostly blanket. Beyond the mist the waterfall crashed into the pool sending spray in all directions.

The noise was thunderous and yet so peaceful.

From where Allegra stood she made out a ledge at the base of the falls, the perfect spot to wash up with the falling sheet of water to screen her for a little bit of privacy.

She gripped her packages and walked along the water's edge until she reached the far wall of the falls. Small hand-holes had been dug into the wall, enabling visitors to climb up if they wished to avoid the path. A precarious climb, but probably fun.

She laid her clothing beside the sloshing water, just far enough away to keep it dry. Then she undressed and—grabbing her towel and soap—slipped a toe into the water to test the temperature.

Pleasantly warm, the water encased her foot in a heated embrace and Allegra entered the pool. She sank deep until the water reached her neck. Holding her items high above her head, she waded across toward the falls and slipped through a gap in the falling sheets of water.

Safely on the ledge, she set the towel against the back wall and edged toward the water, slipping under the spray and encasing herself in hot water.

There must be a geyser somewhere upriver for the falls to be so warm, and Allegra thought they'd come upon a brilliant stroke of luck. The mad rush out of Qusqu had been borderline crazy, enough to set her nerves on edge. This little reprieve was so welcome.

She washed up then lathered her hair, listening to the birds and watching the sun dance on the spray and turn into rainbows.

As she rinsed her hair out a noise filtered through to her, loud enough to hear above the rushing water.

Heart thudding, Allegra peered through the water and saw the outline of a man as he trudged up the path alongside the pool. Wiping her eyes, she sighed with relief as she realized it was Max.

It took a moment for it to dawn on her that she stood naked under the falls and he'd see her as soon as he drew closer.

She was done with her hair, and had a towel wrapped around her when Max slipped inside the alcove.

Stark naked.

Averting her eyes—regretfully though as she really did want to get a good look at his . . . physique—Allegra hurried past him and moved to the lower edge where she sat, dropped the towel and slid into the water.

She left him to his ablutions and enjoyed the warmth of the water within the pool. She didn't want to get out of the water while she knew he could see her.

Men in this day and age were very different about nudity. They revered the male physique which was why it was no surprise that a few groups were lobbying to require participation in the Olympics to require nudity.

Allegra thought the idea ridiculous, especially considering the female participants.

To be honest, as much as she appreciated the male form, the idea of watching hundreds of men prance around naked wasn't something that piqued her fancy.

She liked her men naked, yes, but preferably one at a time.

Speaking of naked men, Allegra swung around as a splash drew her attention. Max must be done. But when she turned she couldn't tell where he was.

She shrieked as his head popped up out of the water two feet from her.

Max laughed, the sound refreshingly relaxed as it echoed around the room. He had a nice smile and she wondered when last she'd seen him this relaxed.

"You picked a brilliant spot," she said, raising her voice a little in order to be heard above the sound of chasing water.

He shook his head. "I chose the waterfall yes, but the heat was a design of nature. There is geyser activity in the region, so I suspect there may have been a few new spouts come up since we set this place up."

Allegra nodded as he swam closer. Her eyes flitted to her towel, a flash of white peeking through the falls. "I think I should get back. I need to get some rest and this water is so relaxing I'm sure I'll be asleep in no time. And Les will be wondering where I am—"

Allegra knew she was babbling and when Max floated closer and ended up right in front of her, she shut her mouth mid-sentence. Paddling backward, she directed her movement toward the falls.

When she climbed up inside the alcove she realized she was in a worse position than before. Within the water she'd been protected and hidden. Now, her nakedness would be in full view of her single admirer who was now climbing up the ledge.

Allegra had just wrapped the towel around her and tucked the flap between her breasts when Max walked up to her. She grabbed his towel and threw it at him over her shoulder.

When she turned around he'd wrapped it around his waist and was standing there, watching her. "I'm sorry. I didn't realize you were . . . shy."

"I'm not shy," she said. And she really wasn't. Not until she'd found herself naked and in the company of this man in particular. She cleared her throat. "I'd better go."

Max nodded and began to follow her. Allegra realized too late that she'd headed in the wrong direction, opposite to the ledge that would take her back the way she'd come. She turned on her heel and found herself chest-to-chest with Max.

She stepped to her left and Max stumbled as he tried to move out of her way. Allegra spun on her heel to grab him, instinct saying she needed to save him in case he fell over the edge.

Instead, she found herself slipping on a patch of smoothed stone.

Warm arms encircled her, spinning her around until her back was to the wall of the alcove.

A sheet of water rained down on them and Allegra grunted, aware now that her towel was soaked. Army issue towels were not as thick as one would have liked.

"Max?" she said prodding his shoulder in order to get him to move back. "Thanks for the save, but you kind of missed the dry landing."

With water rushing over their heads, they both looked to their left where the wall was bone-dry.

Max grinned and Allegra poked his chest this time. Heat had begun to rise between them. Heat which had nothing to do with geysers.

Max's body was up against hers, his warmth covering her, heating her through to her bones. His face was inches from hers and she lifted her chin to stare at him through the shower cascading down on them.

It was inevitable, the way continents collide, the way the sun rises, the way the moon beckons the waves. Max lowered his lips to Allegra's, and she sighed as she opened her mouth to take him in.

He tasted as good as he had the first time they'd kissed in Londinium—which now felt like eons ago.

Max deepened the kiss and Allegra moaned as heat flooded her limbs. Her breathing quickened and soon long slow kisses turned frantic, rushed, desperate.

Allegra's fingers sank into Max's hair as his lips trailed across her cheek, and down her neck where his heated mouth paid homage to the sensitive skin beneath her ear, the long column of her neck and the hollow above her collarbone. He lavished attention on the skin above the towel before searching out her mouth again. She pulled him close, desperate for more as her body throbbed with need.

Max's hand moved away from her waist and settled on her

breast, his large palm laying claim at last. She let out a soft cry and surged toward him as he tugged at the towel.

The sodden piece of material fell to the stone floor as Max pressed up against her body. Allegra lifted her leg, curling her heel around his waist. All she knew was that she wanted more. More of Max.

She heard the birds cry in the distance, heard the rush of the water competing with the thudding of her heart. She felt the heat from their bodies rise, overpowering the warmth of the waterfall.

They moved in a silent rhythm, a timeless song that spoke of desire, of need, of hope and of carnal delight.

A voice at the back of Allegra's mind whispered that perhaps this wasn't a good idea, that he was her protector. There were lines they were both in the process of crossing.

But she batted the intrusive thoughts away and reveled in the feel of this man. For the moment, he belonged entirely to her and she wasn't going to waste a single second thinking about anything but him.

CHAPTER 34

The shadows were lengthening and the clearing had cooled considerably by the time Max and Allegra returned to the cabin in the trees.

Max headed off to the helicopter, probably to oil the blades and such. Which, to Allegra, translated to not reporting to all and sundry—aka Celestra—that they'd just spent over an hour within the heated waters of the rainbow falls.

Together.

Allegra climbed into the cabin to find Les lying on a cot beside a net-covered window, staring out at the clear sky.

She shifted her gaze to Allegra and gave her a small smile. A judgment- and jealousy-free one.

Relieved, Allegra smiled back and the two women set about preparing a meal from a range of tinned food that looked suspiciously like they dated back at least a decade.

Later, Allegra took the path of ignorance being bliss, and ate her fill while attempting to avoid Max's eyes.

After dinner he offered to clean up and as Allegra got comfortable on her cot, Max cleared his throat. "You both need to be ready. We leave as soon as it's dark."

The instruction brooked no argument and Allegra was too tired to complain about lack of rest.

The soak in the mineral-enriched hot water had done wonders for her aching muscles. Sleep took her, pulling her deep within its bone-numbing embrace.

And Allegra passed out like a light.

CHAPTER 35

*A*s much as she'd been afraid of visions or dreams destroying her rest, Allegra found that she'd slept like the dead.

She shuddered at the analogy and pushed herself up on the cot. Beside her Les was already folding her clothing and dusting out the blankets from the cot.

Returning the cabin to its previous state of acceptable tidiness, the three descended only for Allegra to stand agape at the chopper, now taking pride of place in the middle of the clearing, lit by half a dozen torches guarding the site.

Max instructed them to get inside while he attended to the torches, blowing them out and storing them up inside the tree that had once held the chopper. He boarded up the entrance to the cabin and hurried over, climbing inside the chopper.

The two women strapped in and secured the doors as Max began flicking switches. Soon he had the chopper in the air and despite the darkness they made their way out with the jungle beneath them.

Max took the chopper in a wide arch and Allegra stared in awe at the sight of the majestic trees stretching out in the distance, its pure unadulterated wildness lit by the silver light of the moon.

Hours later, when the sky began to change color as the sun crept up on the most distant horizon, Max called out to Allegra.

"We're landing soon," he looked over his shoulder at her, his eyes holding a message for her that went further than a mere arrival announcement.

She nodded even though he'd already turned back to the controls. After waking Les, Allegra readied herself for the landing, then stared out at the horizon. Max banked the chopper left and the aircraft rose over the top of a small mountain, then dipped low, following the undulation of the land.

Max flew across the valley, and even from a distance Allegra could see a compound up ahead. A large villa was built on the hillside, protected by fences and security on all sides.

This was the Pythia Aurelia's home.

Allegra took a deep breath feeling the sense of home within her bones. Was knowing her predecessor had made her home here making Allegra channel that sense of belonging?

She didn't know.

She pushed it deep into her mind as she watched Max land the chopper, watched half a dozen people, including an ancient woman, hurry to the courtyard.

Max helped Allegra and Les alight and beckoned them to follow as he bent slightly forward away from the rushing air of the still spinning rotator blades.

"Ah, Vissarion. What are you doing here?" the old woman croaked as she glared at him, her voice somewhere between teasing affection, and angry irritation.

Max merely smiled at her and bent to kiss her cheek. She narrowed an eye as she looked first at Max and then at Les and Allegra.

Her gaze remained on Allegra for a while and then she smiled, her toothless grin incongruous in the facade of a terrifying old woman.

"Come. I will show you to your room." Allegra wasn't sure if the old woman was talking to her or to Max, but she obeyed anyway.

They were led through the small village and up to the villa where the old woman showed them to a large room.

Beside Allegra, Max's eyes gleamed as they roamed around the room, studying the various items with an easy familiarity.

"You didn't change anything," he asked looking over his shoulder at the old woman.

She snorted. "What do I need to change. It waits for her," she said flicking a finger at Allegra. "If she wants to change, she can change."

After she shooed Max and Les out of the room, Allegra stared at the low soft bed, and the floor-to-ceiling painting on the wall behind it.

Delphi. The temple on the hillside.

If she hadn't already guessed as to whose room she'd been given, she'd certainly know it now.

Allegra turned to watch the old woman watching her.

"Why did you give me her room?"

"Because she would have wanted me to." The old woman moved to the window and pointed at what looked like a large box that performed the task of seat as well as storage trunk.

She pointed at it. "She left this for you."

"For me?"

"You need to know who you are. Aurelia wanted you to have a place to start." The old woman looked over at the door. "You may as well show it to *him* when you are done. He's going to want to strangle me, but please tell him while I am around. I want to see the look in his eye."

"Why? Will he be surprised?"

"More like furious. He's been looking for your past and all he had to do was come looking for it here." The old woman cackled so loudly that Allegra was sure she would choke and laugh herself to death.

Even after the old woman had left her in the room alone, Allegra could still hear her cackling laughter down the hall.

After a while, a younger girl arrived with water and towels, and pointed Allegra to a door to the patio.

To her left was a path and the girl waved her in that direction. Allegra obeyed and followed the dirt track until she came to a small pool. A roof had been built over the pool, and nine columns encircled the water, holding up the rounded roof.

Two women sat inside the pool and both looked up as Allegra drew closer.

They bent their head to each other and whispered words Allegra could not hear.

Then they stood to leave, both casting shy smiles at Allegra who found herself quite relieved they weren't leaving because she was a pariah.

Allegra found herself alone and sank into the waters, glad again for the warmth.

She hurried with her bathing trying to shove out the memories of Max and herself. Refreshed, Allegra returned to the room, now dressed in what she was sure was an ancient—or at least an ancient-styled—hand-beaded Roman dress.

The style was flattering and Allegra enjoyed the comfort of it.

She met Max and Les in the origin area where the two were drinking tall glasses of something making her mouth water.

She accepted a glass and was surprised to find it was an orange and apple blend with a hint of something almost bitter. And alcohol of sorts. One that kicked a bit of a punch.

After a quiet dinner during which Allegra watched Max banter with the old woman—who Max had finally introduced as Mara, Aurelia's handmaiden—she was ready to head to bed.

As she rose, Mara said, "I would like to offer my continued

service to you, Allegra." The cackling laughter that followed made Allegra wonder if she was being tested.

Thankfully she wasn't expected to answer immediately and was relieved to be sent to bed by the bossy old woman.

The night had ended later than Allegra's body had wanted and she'd trudged to her bedroom exhausted.

CHAPTER 36

*T*he next morning Allegra was awakened by the sound of a million birdcalls, and the shrieking of a parrot or two.

Sunlight simmered on the inky horizon as Allegra rose from the bed to sit at the window and watch the pure beauty of nature in this land.

When the golden sunlight had bled its way into the blue darkness, and when the yellow and gold won the battle over darkness and night, Allegra finally sank to the floor and opened the trunk.

The flat lid was patterned with paintings of women and men cavorting, instruments in hand, many resembling the ones she'd seen in her vision of the temple of Apollo in Delphi.

Allegra lifted the lid and wondered at the lack of security for something that seemed to have so much value.

Inside the box was a folded-up length of fabric, the color a faded mink, its edges banded in rusty bronze thread. She lifted it away, curious as to what it was, but more inquisitive about what else the box could hide. What it might hold that Mara had felt was so important for Allegra to see.

Beneath the fabric were stacks of books, and tucked at the back was a large leather envelope overflowing with papers. Allegra scanned the books and found they were diaries, documented experiences of Aurelia's lifetime as well as a few Pythias before her, Cathenna's diary being one of them.

Written in Ancient Greek, it seemed strange that Allegra was able to understand every word, despite her knowledge of the language being more than a little rusty.

Allegra set the diary aside, mentally putting it on the top of her list to go through. Turning her attention back to the box, Allegra's fingers reached for the leather folder of their own accord.

She unwound the leather strap and widened the mouth of the folder, her eyebrows rising at the sight of a thick stack of papers that appeared to range in age from recently mass-produced pulp paper to linen and papyrus, yellowed with age, ink almost translucent in places.

Allegra moved the envelope to the bed and spread out the papers, scanning them to identify a pattern. The common factor among so many of the sheets of paper sent Allegra's heart racing.

Allegra sat back and took another deep breath. Cathenna's death played over and over in her mind, Langcourt's ancestor's cold smile as he stood over her and watched her take her last breaths.

Allegra returned the folder to the chest and was about to close it—feeling a deep ache within her heart at the truth she'd discovered—when something caught her eye.

At the bottom of the trunk was a dagger in a solid metal sheath, the hilt a dull gold studded with gems. Allegra pulled the dagger free and studied the weapon, her eyes widening at the beauty of the blade.

It looked ancient, like something that may have been passed down from Pythias of the past.

Allegra took the dagger and sheath and held the weapon up to the light. She wrapped the belt of the sheath around her hips and slipped the dagger home, absorbing the feel of the weapon against her thigh. She'd never been the type of person to enjoy weapons, and yet for some reason this dagger felt right at home at her hip.

She leaned forward and checked if there was anything else.

One item remained. A folder bound in leather and edged in brass, was a very official folder. Allegra opened it slowly, wary of what lay inside, and revealed a pristine white card marked with a short narrow row of lines that varied in width. The card was attached to a piece of paper with a paperclip, only one made of a bright silvery metal unlike the more common bronzed ridged types Allegra was familiar with.

She shifted the card off the paper and studied the details.

The name on the first line was printed in clear letters, although Allegra wasn't sure what type of typewriter could create a printed letter so clean and sharp.

Her heart thudded as she absorbed this information.

ALLEGRA JOCASTA DAMASKOS

WHO ELSE COULD it be besides Allegra herself? Was this her birth certificate? And if so, what did it mean?

She stared at the date of birth and shook her head. With trembling fingers, she closed the leather folder and placed it at the bottom of the trunk.

Allegra shut the trunk and sank onto the lid. She leaned over, exhaustion pulling at her limbs again, filling her mind like a fog.

She rested her elbows on her knees, then dropped her head into her open palms. Massaging her skull she tried to understand what the birth certificate meant, and what Aurelia meant in leaving it for her to see.

At last she got to her feet and smoothed down the front of her nightdress. The floor was cool beneath her feet as she went into the small bathroom that sat off the room.

After her morning routine, she changed and headed downstairs in search of some form of sanity.

CHAPTER 37

*M*ara's idea of giving Allegra something to do was so far removed from what Allegra had expected that she'd failed the first task outright.

She'd followed Mara all the way to the bottom of the hill and found herself surprised that the grounds, which had been empty yesterday, were now filled with sparring men and women.

Mara had directed Allegra to one end where a tall woman—whose bulging biceps glinted in the afternoon sun—waited.

Mara whispered something to the woman and then headed past Allegra, giving her a grin. Later, Allegra wondered how she hadn't seen through the old woman before that.

As she turned to face her opponent she felt something hit hard on the back of her legs and sweep her off her feet.

Allegra landed flat on her back, staring up at the clear blue sky.

So much for all the martial arts training during her formative years.

She'd expected laughter from the other trainees but she received only silence. Apart from Mara's self-satisfied cackling.

The afternoon passed with Allegra leaving the training grounds, her arms and thighs covered in black-and-blue welts.

An hour immersed in the hot pools was sufficient to ease her pains and Allegra entered the dining-room, a smile on her face and a spring in her step.

"That smile does not match the condition of your body," said Les as she filled her plate with slices of chicken.

"As incongruous as it sounds, I have never felt better."

"She is a natural," said Mara as she hobbled into the room. The old woman seemed slower now, despite how well she'd bested Allegra on the field not too long ago. Mara snorted as she caught Allegra's scrutiny. "It's not about how much you fight, but more about how well you fight."

Allegra nodded, finding herself agreeing with the old woman. She bit back a retort, the urge to inform the old woman that she was experienced enough. Still Mara was likely to insult her training considering she'd been trounced by a woman almost 4 times her age.

As she took her seat she felt the photograph crinkle in the pocket of her skirt. Through dinner the piece of paper seemed to burn a hole into her thighs and she was supremely glad when the meal came to an end.

As the after-dinner conversation shifted into a lull of companionable silence, Allegra drew the photograph out of her pocket and placed it in front of Les and Mara who were both sitting opposite her and Max.

Both women stilled and Allegra found herself confused. She glanced up and met Max's eyes. He too seemed intrigued by the women's seemingly mirrored consternation at the sight of Langcourt's face.

Mara looked up first.

"So you know him?" asked Allegra.

Mara nodded and was about to speak when Allegra shook her head, looking pointedly at Les who looked up only a fraction slower.

"Recognize him?"

Les nodded. "I know him. I saw him at a meeting the ambassador had with General Qhapaq."

"Do you usually go to meetings with McIvor?" asked Max.

Another nod. "Especially when it has to do with community or citywide events. It was a planning session in preparation of the New Year celebrations. We were meant to talk about budgets and what the NGS Embassy planned to contribute."

Les paused as she picked up the photo and stared at the image. "He was there, in the general's office. Whatever he'd had to discuss it had taken longer than expected, and we found ourselves waiting almost thirty minutes. Then he came out fuming about something . . . barely looked at us as he left. It's why I remember him. He was very, very creepy and far too arrogant when most people are extremely deferential with the general. Qhapaq's too powerful a man to anger in any way."

Allegra sat back, biting on her lip as she absorbed the knowledge that the man who had tortured her was in Qusqu right now.

She glanced over at Mara who nodded solemnly.

"If you ever see this man, I suggest you run. Far, and fast. You do not want to encounter him, no matter how powerful you think you are."

"Who is he?" Allegra asked, wanting to know what Mara herself knew of Langcourt.

"Lord Severus Langcourt. Or at least that's the name he's been going by during the last . . . recently." Her gaze shifted briefly to Les who was still staring at the photograph. "Whatever you do, do not engage him. Stay away." She nodded at the scar on Allegra's chest. "I will not be surprised to find he was behind your attempted assassination. The man is very adept and determined when it comes to removing the Pythian line from existence."

Les stared up at Allegra as Mara spoke. "What do you mean removing the Pythian line?"

Allegra leaned forward. "He's a very dangerous man. Did you hear any of what they were discussing?"

Les shook her head. "No. I wasn't listening because the ambassador was talking the entire time. We could hear raised voices at one point but then nothing. He left in a rush, seemed angry."

Max grunted. "I'm surprised he made a visit to the general in public."

"Desperate?" suggested Allegra.

Max nodded. "Very likely." He took a deep breath and got to his feet. "I need to retire. I have a few things to sort before bed." He looked at Allegra. "You need to get some rest. I'm not sure how much battle training is going to help you when you need to rest and recuperate."

He threw Mara a glare that said volumes.

As he walked off, Allegra gave Mara an apologetic smile and followed after Max. She met him at the top of the stairs and he paused to wait for her.

"You don't approve of the training?"

He shook his head. "I think it's a good idea. But not at this particular point in time. The doctors said you needed rest."

"And you think trekking through the jungle was resting?"

"That couldn't be helped. And it was probably not the best idea especially coming so soon after being shot. I just worry you aren't getting enough rest to recover properly."

Allegra stepped closer to him and placed her palm on his chest. "I'm fine. I promise." She could feel the beat of his heart beneath her fingers.

She felt Max's arms wrap around her as he tucked her head under his chin, enveloping her within his warmth. "Just as long as you tell me if you are not."

She nodded, her head bobbing and bumping into his chin. She wanted to stay there within his arms for as long as possible, but a noise at the bottom of the stairs drew her attention.

Mara stood below them, her pale eyes staring up at them. Allegra moved away from Max. Her smile was wide and cheeky and she cackled as she said, "Aurelia will be happy." Then she grinned again, "Have you told her?" She nodded at Allegra.

Max remained silent.

"Very well. When the time is right, eh?" she laughed and began to walk off. As her footsteps receded Allegra heard her say, "Wait too long and it might be too late."

Allegra looked up at Max, and her heart tightened at the expression on his face; conflict, confusion, and a touch of fear.

She smiled and patted his arm. "I told you, I am happy for you to wait until you felt the time is right. And I meant it."

Allegra left him standing there and hurried down the hall. As she reached her room she turned and looked over her shoulder, giving him a reassuring smile.

"I can wait. Don't worry about Mara."

She spoke the words and found she meant it, because she'd discovered one crucial truth.

She trusted Max.

CHAPTER 38

*M*ax clenched his fingers into fists as he glared down at the photograph in his hand. He'd kept the image with him, but now he wasn't so sure why he'd taken it.

It wasn't as if he didn't know who Langcourt was. The Brittanic police had given the NGS and FAPA a report on their raid of the tunnels and the grounds where Allegra had been held. At the time neither Max nor the Brittanic police had known who the High Priest was.

Only after the raid, and the torching of the ancient Langcourt villa, did the Brittanic police confirm the ownership of the estate and surrounding land. Langcourt had gone missing—presumed dead—and the Brittanic police were happy to put the case to bed.

And why would they not have been happy? One of their most illustrious lords, a man from a family whose history went back generations, was under suspicion of heading up a cult responsible for killing and mutilating children.

Max and Allegra had left Londinium so quickly, on the trail of a deadly virus, that they hadn't been there to receive the report first hand.

The high priest's suspected identity as Lord Severus Langcourt was confirmed, but since then he'd gone AWOL and nobody had seen him since.

And now he turns up in Qusqu, the very same place Allegra had seen the destruction of an entire city.

Was it mere coincidence that he was here, or was there some fated design to the whole disaster?

Max brought up the mail program on his phone and typed in the details of everything that had transpired over the last few days, from the blowing up of their embassy apartment to their escape, and then the destruction of their getaway chopper. When he got to the trek through the jungle and Les's betrayal he paused, still unable to believe Les would do such a thing. What was motivating her, he had no idea. Not that he could claim to know her anymore anyway.

One thing Max was sure of; he'd been careful about the circuitous route he'd taken, and he'd stayed below radar. He was pretty certain they hadn't been followed but he could very well be wrong.

Given that he'd had no clue they'd been followed the first time, and had been blindsided when their pursuers had shot the first chopper out of the sky, Max wasn't about to get complacent.

He sent a message to Marcus requesting immediate backup to be sent to Qusqu. Only when he got the confirmation that they were coming did he relax. He filled Marcus in on the danger to McIvor and possible danger to his wife. Their safety was of great concern which warranted a quicker response from the NGS. He didn't say anything further about his suspicions regarding the McIvors' possible involvement.

It irked Max that the McIvors would get the NGS moving faster than the Pythia could. Suppressing a sigh Max headed for the bed. While Allegra had been training with Mara and her team, he'd been servicing the chopper. Having sat so long unused, Max was surprised the old Bell army chopper was still in excellent condition. He wanted to be fueled, serviced and ready to go as soon as possible.

He'd brought Allegra here for safety, but knowing what they knew now, safety was a luxury they couldn't afford.

BREAKFAST WAS a subdued affair and Max waited until the moment was right to make his announcement.

"You cannot be serious," Les whispered setting her glass of peach tea down on the table with a thump.

"I'm dead serious. We have no choice. Sitting here doing nothing is worse than going back and trying to save the city."

Les shook her head. "You have no idea what you're doing."

Max grinned. "Maybe I don't, but I'm not going to do nothing, either. Langcourt will come for Allegra no matter where she is. You can stay here with Mara and the team. Nobody knows you're here so you'll be safe."

Les was shaking her head but Max had already turned his attention to Allegra. "I can see you're feeling better."

"Must be those magical waters. They seem to rejuvenate me every time I soak myself in it."

Her eyes widened and Mara let out a bark of laughter. "Don't worry. These are not magical waters. They are just full of minerals. Copper, magnesium, zinc. All good things for the rejuvenation of muscles."

Max nodded, his expression saying he was barely paying Mara any attention. "We should be heading back soon. I'd like to leave at sundown."

Mara nodded then looked over at Allegra, her smile warm— unusual for the old cantankerous woman. "You must return soon."

Allegra was shaking her head, unsure if there would be a need in the future to return. A part of her thought it wouldn't be such a bad idea. She'd quite enjoyed herself at the compound.

Mara smiled. "This is your home now. Aurelia left the compound and the responsibility of all its people to you as the new Pythia."

Allegra's mouth dropped open and she had to force it shut. A sense of belonging filled her, warring with the responsibility now within her hands.

The knowledge that the place now belonged to her put Allegra under a great deal of strain. She'd never been responsible for other people before and she wasn't sure she was up to the task. And yet she was unable to turn the old woman down.

Allegra merely nodded and got to her feet, readying herself to head to her room and pack.

They took the next two hours to prepare and Mara bade them farewell in front of the open door of the chopper.

The old woman patted her cheek, and bent close to whisper words in her ear.

As the chopper left the ground and ascended, Allegra stared at Mara through the glass.

"Go with the grace of Apollo, Allegra Damascus."

Allegra was sure the old woman had pronounced her surname as Damaskos.

CHAPTER 39

*T*he flight back to Qusqu was filled with silence, only relieved when they stopped at the waterfall to refuel for the last leg of the journey.

Les had decided on returning with Allegra and Max, but she behaved as if they were forcing her. She sat in a huff, glaring out of the window, it annoyed Allegra to no end.

"Why did you come if you didn't want to? Nobody forced you," Allegra said, then gritted her teeth. She wanted to say so much more but she felt she'd already said too much.

Les snapped her gaze back to Allegra's face. "You have no clue what's going on. I have too much at stake," she bit out before her eyes widened.

Allegra assumed now that Les may have slipped and said too much. "Les, what's going on? What are you not telling us?" Allegra probed, hoping Les would reveal a little more. "We brought you away for your own safety, but you haven't been honest with us about what's really going on."

Les's jaw tightened and she turned away, staring out of the window now. "I've said enough."

Allegra wanted to continue the questioning but she'd learned a thing or two about Les. When the woman made a decision, no matter how much she didn't like it, she kept to it. And now, it meant that no matter what Allegra said or did, she wouldn't get anything out of Les.

CHAPTER 40

*M*ax touched down in a field a few miles out of Qusqu and they were met by two cars, army issue all-terrain vehicles with roll bars and gigantic wheels.

Max's gut was tight, but he'd pulled a steady calm over his thoughts. There were too many possible options to consider and he needed to focus. He felt bombarded from so many sides. With just him to protect both Allegra and Les he found himself feeling a little impotent.

The soldiers ushered them into the vehicles and drove them to a drop point a few minutes outside the city where they stopped to drop the three off at a parked car.

Again, the NGS team was efficient, giving them clothing and hats to wear that would at least partially protect their identity. They entered the city pretending to be tourist types. Max was driving them to a safe house, one owned by FAPA that sat on the outskirts of the city, as far from the ruined embassy building as they could get.

"Let's move inside and we can figure out what we're doing next," said Max. His words were completely unnecessary and he had a suspicion he was speaking only in order to fill the silence.

Les, who'd been stiff and silent most of the way, stalked off into the building without a word.

"Don't worry about her. She'll calm down," Max murmured as they grabbed their bags and followed her.

Allegra shrugged. "Something is going on that she isn't willing to share. I wish I could help her, but either she can't tell us or she won't tell us. I'm more sure now than ever that she's being blackmailed or controlled somehow. That whatever she is doing is against her will and she has no choice."

Max paused as he held the door open for her. "You really think so?"

"She just appears very conflicted to me. But you know her better than I do. What does her behavior tell you?"

Max sighed. "To tell you the truth I can no longer read her. Whatever is going on in her head, it's not something I can understand. And neither is it something she is willing to tell me about."

They entered the apartment and Max scanned the street before he shut the door behind them.

Allegra set her duffel on the floor. "Well, whatever it is I have a bad feeling about it."

"You and me both," said Max.

As she walked toward the room Max called out, "Wait. One more thing."

She turned on her heel, a smile on her face. She looked uncertain, as if she wasn't sure what she'd been expecting, and the long narrow jewel box he held out to her was not it.

"What's this for?"

"It's an emergency distress beacon."

Flipping the lid her eyes widened. A narrow bracelet glinted up at her, a long band of diamonds and multicolored gems that was both elegant and attractive. A heart-shaped charm hung from the clasp.

Marcus had had it delivered to the embassy while Allegra had been unconscious, and Max felt she needed it now. Things were too insane to be complacent.

"Press the carved portion—it's the switch—and it will send out the emergency transmission. It will allow us to find you provided you activate it while near enough so I can get a lock on you first. Otherwise, it will be like looking for a needle in a haystack."

Allegra smiled and nodded, tucking the box into her bag. She left him then, and he couldn't help but notice the worry in her eyes.

He stood there for a moment in the darkened living room, immersed in worry for what could happen tomorrow. Then he forced himself to move, to check the property and confirm everything was safely locked down, to check on the guards posted discretely on nearby street corners.

He'd covered all his bases to ensure their safety.

Or at least he hoped he had.

CHAPTER 41

$\mathcal{A}$ few hours later, they retired to their rooms, fatigue from their travels weighing them all down. Les's behavior hadn't changed. In fact, Allegra got the distinct feeling the other woman's attitude had only grown worse.

Allegra had attempted to draw Les into the conversion once or twice during their meal and after receiving silence in response, she'd decided it was best to let the other woman be.

Allegra lay in her bed, suffocated by the silence. The building they were housed in was more of a modern villa style, very unlike the embassy pyramid. For some reason, Allegra felt insecure about the location and found herself unable to sleep.

Something rattled in the living area outside her room and she sat up on the bed, straining to pick out any further sounds.

She heard it again, a soft scrape that could have been anything, a heel on a tile, or a knife on glass.

Dressing quickly, she slipped the dagger holster around her waist and got to her feet before tiptoeing to her door. She was just about to open it when everything went crazy.

People were yelling, and Allegra heard Les scream. From the

sound of the footsteps Allegra guessed there were at least half a dozen intruders in the apartment.

She turned on her heel, desperately scanning the room for a way out but the only window in the room bore shadows of people standing a little too close to the glass. They were about to come in through the window *and* the door and Allegra wasn't sure exactly what she was supposed to do. She wasn't planning on hiding though.

She moved to the other side of the room, away from both the door and the window, and waited, feeling the weight of the dagger at her hip.

Allegra didn't take the dagger in her hand yet. Time seemed to slow as she waited for the door to slam open. Or for the window to shatter.

Two masked men stormed into the room, flashlights sweeping left and right.

"Stay where you are," the first one yelled so loudly that Allegra raised an eyebrow as his gruff voice grated on her ears.

"I'm not deaf," she said, remaining still.

The man ignored her words, just kept his weapon trained on her while his silent partner searched the room, his thin tall frame slipping into the shadows.

The shadowy intruder got back onto his feet after searching under the bed—what for, Allegra had no clue—and immediately ducked as someone came flying through the window.

Whoever they were, they were wobbly and unsteady on their feet and clearly had little to no combat skill. The only thing they had was the element of surprise.

And a good weapon.

The third intruder—Wobbly—raised his weapon and shot Thin Man, the barrel of the gun shaking dangerously.

Despite his wild aim Wobbly managed to take Thin Man down, then pointed the weapon at Gruff whose gun was still aimed at Allegra's chest while his attention remained focused on the barrel of the gun in his face.

Allegra lunged forward and grabbed the long barrel of the gun. She pulled hard, tipping Gruff sideways, and he stumbled. He'd been concentrating on Wobbly and couldn't regain his balance in time.

He hit the ground hard. As he was turning over to get back up, two shots rang out and he fell back onto the floor, deathly still. In the dark, Allegra couldn't see any wounds, or any blood for that matter.

What she could see was the barrel of a gun pointed directly at her face.

"Drop it," Wobbly said.

Allegra let go of the gun and winced as it hit the floor with a clatter.

"Move," he motioned with the gun and Allegra was forced to slide past him in the direction of the window.

As she approached the window sill, Allegra reached for the bracelet Max had given her and pressed the front of the small heart charm. Hopefully the tracking beacon would work and Max would be able to find her where she was taken. Now, she had no choice but to throw a leg over the sill and jump out of the window, especially considering the barrel of the gun pressed into her spine.

As she landed on the ground she tensed. Wobbly was in the process of climbing out of the window, giving her ample opportunity to make a run for it.

"Don't even think about it," came a voice that sent chills up and down Allegra's spine.

The sound of Langcourt's voice sent ice straight into Allegra's bones, but it didn't have the effect he'd no doubt been expecting.

A red rage filled her as memories flooded back, of the pain, of the whips as they hit her back and ripped open her skin.

She spun on her heel and lashed out at him, blindly reacting to a pent-up fury that surprised even herself.

Her hand connected with his chin and sent him hard into the wall beside him. His skull made a hollow thunking sound as it hit and bounced off the stone.

Langcourt let out an angry growl and reached for Allegra. In her peripheral vision, she saw Langcourt's accomplice struggling to get out through the window, the length of his rifle caught on the upper edge of the window frame jamming him in position. Wobbly and useless.

It would have been funny if Langcourt hadn't been trying to kill her.

She swung her arm wide, hitting her wrist downward onto Langcourt's forearm. As his hand fell she reached out and grabbed his wrist, intending to pull him toward her and knee him in the crotch—a move she'd perfected when she'd first begun her training.

But the best-laid plans were always made before being broken.

Allegra's fingers closed around Langcourt's wrist. And the street, and the two men around her fell away into darkness.

CHAPTER 42

$\mathcal{A}$llegra opened her eyes to find herself lying on an icy stone floor, the right half of her body numb with cold.

She lifted her head, feeling the tight muscles in her neck complain, but she ignored them. She had to get up, get moving.

Just her luck that she'd end up having a vision when Langcourt was trying to abduct her.

She shivered at the memory but thrust it from her mind. She couldn't deal with that reality right now. There were more important things she had to consider. Like where in Apollo's name was she?

Sitting upright she blinked against the shadows, trying to make out the room around her. It appeared little more than a stone cell, although the window was wide and very large.

Allegra scrambled to her feet, half-crawling-half-limping to the window, her heart thudding with the prospect of escape. All she had to do was get out of the building and run as fast as she could.

She slammed into the ledge, her legs giving way too quickly. And her heart sank as she stared out at a panoramic view of a jungle.

In the daylight.

Early morning light seeped in at the horizon and the trilling of birds undulated on the air. She'd been unconscious for too long.

She prayed the tracking chip in her bracelet had worked and Max had been able to follow Langcourt to the pyramid, wherever in the Qusquan jungle they happened to be.

Boosting herself onto her stomach she peered over the ledge and let out a soft cry of disappointment. The pyramid was old and huge, and had been left to run into disrepair. Moss and lichen covered the stone while creeping vines wended their way up to the top of the structure, as if intent on swallowing the pyramid whole.

The room she was in—though not very high up— jutted out slightly, making it clear that escape would be a death-defying act. Something Allegra wasn't afraid to try.

From somewhere nearby, somewhere within the jungle below, Allegra heard the cry of a jaguar, a low reverberating roar she felt in her bones.

She peered below and watched as the large feline—as dark as night, eyes glinting bright gold—paced at the base of the pyramid.

Great. The guard was a killer predator. Neither bribery nor seduction would work on the animal. Allegra sighed and turned to face the locked door.

As she closed in on it she was surprised to find her weapon was still strapped to her hip. Her captors must be extremely confident to leave her armed. Or they had no idea she could wield it well enough to defend herself.

Of course, her dagger was nothing in the face of their guns.

Before she could decide what to do, the door opened and Langcourt walked inside, his hands behind his back as he began to pace in front of her.

"My dear girl. You are certainly more trouble than you are

worth." He smiled, his teeth glinting in the moonlight. "Although, passing out at the most convenient moment certainly helped."

Allegra hid a smirk. So he had no idea she'd had a vision. Well, she could work with that. She glared at him, bringing anger to the surface easily when it came to this man. "Thanks to you trying to kill me," she spat the words at him, her voice filled with venom. "Maybe you should have done the job properly the first time."

Langcourt smiled, his expression that of a patient father reprimanding an unruly child. "I'm afraid you are quite mistaken my dear. Neither I nor my employees, are responsible for that unfortunate incident. I was very clear in that you were to be brought to me unharmed."

"They didn't listen, did they?'

He shrugged. "I will endeavor to find out who is responsible—"

"I think you know who it was," Allegra snapped, her voice filled with accusation. She hoped he would be fooled but she couldn't be sure. Not when she knew now what he was truly capable of.

"I have a suspicion."

"Qhapaq?"

Langcourt's eyebrows rose a tiny fraction and then he gave her an innocent look. "I'm afraid I don't know who this person is?"

"I am afraid I am not fooled by you," she shot back. "I know you met the general and I know you're planning something with him."

"Did one of your visions tell you this?" Allegra remained silent, wanting him to come to whatever conclusion his mind took him to. "Well, that's a pity. Your visions are becoming problematic. It's a good thing I finally have my hands on you. Now I'm hoping you will no longer be a problem for me."

Allegra was about to ask him how he planned on doing that

when footsteps in the corridor drew her attention. A cloaked man, his Qullan features clear even beneath his hood, paused on the threshold. "It is time."

Langcourt sniffed and straightened as if annoyed at the interruption. Still, he nodded at the man. "I'll be on my way." His tone dismissed the man, but moments later the guard still remained in the doorway.

Langcourt looked at him. "I said—"

"I was told to wait with you. You are needed immediately."

Langcourt huffed but complied, walking toward the door. Over his shoulder he said, "I'll be back soon. We have much to discuss."

"That's what you think," mumbled Allegra to herself.

The door shut behind him with a heavy clunking sound that made Allegra wince. How would she ever get past that? She felt like she was locked inside the money vault of a bank.

Sighing, she spun on her heel and let out a shriek. Covering her mouth with one hand Allegra froze in position as she stared at the jaguar which now stood on the top of the balcony ledge. The creature watched Allegra, her almond eyes glinting, her black pelt shimmering in the pale moonlight.

Was this how she would die? Was this the end that Langcourt had in mind for her? It didn't make sense. From what Allegra knew of the man, he liked to do his own dirty work. And if not, he liked to be there to see the job done. That made Allegra certain that if anything, the jaguar was there to keep an eye on her, to make sure she didn't escape.

Jaguar guard dog.

The great cat moved, her shoulder undulating as she took one more step then jumped off the ledge and onto the floor just inside the window.

Allegra swallowed hard. Was she going to be jaguar dinner?

Allegra took a step away and soon found herself backed up against the far wall.

She wanted to chase the cat away but she wasn't sure 'shoo' would do the job. Instead she remained still, her hand on the hilt of her dagger. As stunningly beautiful as the jaguar was, Allegra had no qualms about using her dagger against the creature in order to prevent an attack. Or in order to save herself from being eaten.

The jaguar came to a stop in the middle of the room and lifted its head high. Before Allegra could voice her fear, the body of the jaguar began to shimmer. Blue and silver lights glinted across the midnight pelt and then faded away, leaving behind the form of a naked woman.

A woman Allegra knew all too well.

"Athena?" Allegra frowned as she stared at Chief Inspector Nostrus, confused but not surprised at the sudden transformation of cat to woman.

"You're not surprised?" Athena asked as she reached around her neck to unclasp a narrow silk pouch.

Allegra shook her head, watching Athena remove something from the pouch; a garment perhaps. "I've seen some insane things in the last few months. This wasn't as bad as some of them."

Athena laughed softly and dusted out the folded silk to reveal a black pantsuit. "I'm sure you have had a few strange experiences." She stepped into the suit and slid the sleeves onto her shoulders. Allegra was impressed at the woman's ingenuity. "My Lady, I'm sorry if I gave you a fright."

"Not scared at all."

Athena laughed again. "I have feline hearing, remember?"

Allegra smiled and pushed off the wall. "Is this a rescue mission?"

"That it is," the chief inspector murmured as she studied the cell. "They certainly don't provide decent accommodation here."

Athena headed to the door and tried the handle, but the thick metal wouldn't budge. She gave it a nod, as if accepting that it was not going to be their escape route.

Allegra shook her head and headed for the window sill. "So, what are you? A shapeshifter?"

Athena followed and shook her head. "I am daughter of Itzpa-palotl, ancient goddess of creation and death. I can take the form of most warm-blooded animals. But I prefer the jaguar over most others. It makes me feel closest to my mother."

"I thought she took the form of a butterfly?" asked Allegra.

"You know your mythology?"

Allegra nodded. "Fascinated by it," she said dryly.

The demigod smiled. "Yes. My mother takes the form of a butterfly but she is of course partial to jaguar claws. As her child, I get to choose my animal form." Athena boosted herself up on the ledge and motioned for Allegra to follow. "I can leave here easily enough but you have to climb. I can help you, but you're going to have to use your strength."

Allegra nodded. Rolling her shoulders back she said, "What now?"

"Now we climb." Athena pointed at the ledge above their heads. "This balcony extends out of the pyramid itself. We need to get up there in order to walk along the step of the pyramid."

"Then we just descend the steps?"

"Wish it was that easy. We can only go so far until we have to enter the building and look for the internal passages for a way out."

"Why can't we just slide down the side of the pyramid."

Athena shook her head. "A few hundred years ago the emperor who owned this pyramid planted a poisonous creeper along the bottom of the structure. Not much chance of getting out that way."

"Poisonous to humans only, I presume." Allegra was concentrating on reaching up for the ledge when she felt Athena grab her by the waist and lift her up.

Now I was not expecting that.

SHE GRABBED the ledge and drew herself up, and watched as Athena sprang onto the ledge with the same power and grace she possessed in her jaguar form.

Athena dusted her hands and beckoned Allegra as she walked along the narrow step of the pyramid. Here the wall was broken every few feet, gouges and dents of varying sizes pockmarked the stone.

"What happened here?" Allegra asked as she maneuvered across the damaged stone steps.

"A war. Four centuries ago." Athena sounded distracted so Allegra remained silent until they came to a gap in the stone. Here the step of the pyramid had been destroyed, leaving an open space too wide to jump easily. Above, the face of the pyramid was smooth making it clear there was no way out that way.

Allegra was about to turn around to check if the way back was clear when Athena said, "Here, take my hand. I'll swing you across."

"What?"

"You can't make the jump under your own steam, but I have the strength to give you a boost. I can swing you across the open space and all you have to do it catch onto the other ledge. Chances are, if we time it well, you can land directly onto the step."

Allegra lifted her eyebrows but decided she was better off saying nothing. She shifted closer until she faced Athena, her back to the wide open jungle.

Athena took her hands, gripping Allegra's wrists tightly, the way she'd seen gymnasts and aerial performers do.

"I'm going to drop you over the edge so you hang down. Then I'm going to swing you left and right to get some momentum going. I'll say 'on three' when I feel we have a good speed."

Allegra nodded. She knew she was putting her life in Athena's hands but she also knew she had little choice. Her time was limited and she had to get out of the place before Langcourt returned.

As Athena lowered her hands, Allegra gripped tight and allowed herself to drop slowly over the edge. Using her biceps she performed a pull-up, then lowered herself to hang straight down.

Athena nodded and began to swing her left and right, left and right. Allegra kept an eye on the ledge on the opposite side of the chasm, concentrating on the spot she wanted to land on.

At last Athena swung her almost parallel to the step and said, "On three." Allegra took a deep breath and held it as the demigod used her knees to push her strength into the throw. Allegra soon found herself flying through the air and aimed her body directly at the step. She was flexible enough and breathed a sigh of relief as she landed and dropped into a short roll before coming up on her feet smoothly.

When she glanced over at Athena she found the demigod smiling proudly. "You didn't say you were that limber."

Allegra shrugged. "Martial arts from a young age." What she didn't mention was her recent bout of training with Mara, which she realized now had been invaluable.

Athena made the jump smoothly and landed beside Allegra before slipping past to lead the way. They continued until they found a space where they were able to drop down onto the next step.

"I would have expected an even ledge, a proper stepped pyramid."

"The rulers adjusted their pyramid build through the ages. They countered for how easy it was to scale a pyramid by using longer drops between the steps, then added features to make it even more difficult to get into. This is one of the easiest to climb."

Allegra lifted her eyebrows. *This* was easy? She was soaked through with perspiration and the muscles of her upper arms burned with the effort. She felt like she'd been doing pull-ups for hours. Even so, they had managed to descend more than half way down.

They'd reached a window similar to the one that had led to Allegra's cell and the two women flattened themselves against the cantilevered balcony, then shuffled forward to peer over the edge and down into the space.

The wide balcony was empty but the sounds of humming and chanting drifted toward them.

"This is the nearest exit. The other one is on the other side of the pyramid," whispered Athena.

Allegra nodded and watched as Athena somersaulted over the edge swinging backward to drop into the balcony. Allegra, though tempted, didn't follow suit. Instead, she sank into a crouch, held onto the ledge and swung herself down, landing in a crouch facing Athena who stood at the doorway staring inside.

Again, Allegra stared at her bracelet praying Max had picked up the signal. She glanced out over the balcony and stared out at the jungle, trying as hard as she could to see between the trees.

She shook her head. If they came then it would be good, but she wasn't going to wait around for them. She went to stand beside Athena and found they were on a narrow balcony, with a view to a large ceremonial hall below.

Not a ceremonial hall, Allegra corrected herself.

A sacrificial chamber.

CHAPTER 43

*A*llegra watched the ceremony, her mouth open in shock at the sight. Torches blazed all around the room and more than a dozen people stood in a large circle, their heads covered in terrifying masks, their bodies bared and glistening. They wore loincloths, but Allegra could tell almost half of them were women, their oiled breasts glinting in the light.

At one end of the hall on a raised dais, a tall priest held a dagger over the supine body of a young man who lay on a large stone table. The victim stared up at the ceiling, chanting words unfamiliar to Allegra.

She swallowed a gasp as the priest drove the knife deep into the man's chest and made a long incision. The victim continued to chant though his pitch had taken on a pained resonance.

After a few strokes with the blade the priest reached into the chest of the victim and tugged hard. Blood spurted, splashing the wall beyond him, as well as coating the floor around him.

He turned and held the still-beating heart of the victim in his hand, shouting out more words Allegra couldn't understand.

She glanced over at Athena who pulled her back onto the balcony.

"That's not what I expected to see," she whispered.

"What?" asked Allegra both horrified and curious at the bloody sacrifice.

Athena tipped her head at the scene and both women crept back to their vantage point.

The high priest lowered the heart which was beating its last, and bit into it with gusto while the gathered worshipers continued to chant.

Blood ran down the sides of his mouth and dribbled across his chest. His hands were red too, covered in the blood of the victim. And as Allegra studied the rest of the scene she swallowed a gasp.

The blood seeping from the wound of the victim ran from the sacrificial table onto the floor, filling a series of cracks on the ground. From where they stood it was clear the channels had been deliberately carved in order for the blood to reveal the image of an ancient god.

"Which god is it?" she asked softly.

"Pillan," Athena responded, her tone filled with horror. "No," she whispered.

"What's wrong?" Allegra asked, then wanted to laugh hysterically. What was wrong? A man had just ripped out the beating heart of a sacrificial victim and had just eaten it before her very eyes.

"Pillan. He's the god of the Underworld. Of destruction. Of earthquakes and floods. He's the most powerful of all the gods. Storms, disease, war. You name it, he is in charge."

"That is so no good."

"It is worse. The ceremony is to bring him to life in a mortal form." Athena pointed. "The glow is his power slowly coming to life."

Allegra studied the green, almost emerald glow shimmering within the cracks as if coming from beneath the bloody lines.

"Right. That is worse." Allegra took a breath and watched as the priest descended to stand in the very center of the room, raising his hands to the dark ceiling above as he yelled out his chant. "Maybe we should get out of here. Call the authorities."

Athena nodded. "I'll get them out here as soon as possible."

Allegra felt awful for the victims. "That poor man. I wish we could have stopped it."

"There isn't anything you can do. They will keep sourcing victims. This ritual is one in which the sacrifice must be willing. And there are many who would feel honored to be on the table."

"Surely not," Allegra said, not wanting the demigod to be right.

Athena pointed to the dais, at the sacrificial table. "Look beyond the table. Within the shadows."

Allegra followed the direction in which her finger was aimed and pulled away from the doorway fast. She let out a soft cry, glad she'd hidden herself before the sound had escaped.

She blinked, wishing she could unsee the horror. Beyond the table, hidden in the shadows were piles of bodies. At least a dozen dead men and women had been sacrificed in this place, probably only minutes before Allegra and Athena had arrived.

She blinked as she took a breath. Athena came to stand at her side. "Are you going to be all right?" she asked.

Allegra nodded. "Yes. It's just . . . It all makes sense now. The vision. The destruction of the city. This summoning is going to go very wrong very fast. If we allow them to complete the ritual the entire city of Qusqu will sink into the earth and disappear. All that will be left will be a hole in the ground."

"This sounds very much like the actions of Pillan. The consequences of bringing him to this world. The price of resurrecting a god is often too much to pay." The goddess stared at Allegra for a moment and then nodded. "We need to stop them."

The two women moved slowly to the edge of the balcony and studied the gathering. Allegra was about to ask Athena if she felt the high priest resembled Qhapaq when her attention fell on one of the priests. His skin was pale, his belly a bit pronounced. Allegra was almost certain he was Langcourt.

Was this what he had been summoned for?

But before she could mention to Athena that she knew the man, a disturbance at the entrance to the hall below drew her attention.

For a moment, Allegra's heart thundered as she wondered if it was Max they were bringing into the sacrificial chamber. She found herself relieved to see their next victim was not Max, although his identity sent a ripple of shock through Allegra's bones

Ambassador Liam McIvor.

CHAPTER 44

The worshippers surrounding McIvor and the priest began to sway and then move anti-clockwise, chanting louder and louder. McIvor's eyes were round, terrified as he stared at the people encircling him. Allegra's beat fast and she whispered, "I feel like I've seen this before."

Athena gave her an odd look, then turned her attention back to the proceedings. But Allegra couldn't shake the feeling of familiarity.

Flashes of images, people walking back and forth, tall men and women in headdresses, chests bared and oiled. Firelight flickered beyond what she was able to see, the light dancing and reflecting against long iron tipped spears.

Allegra suppressed a gasp. "I *have* seen this before."

She stared at the spears remembering how much the sight of them had impacted her. Hand-carved metal spear-heads, ancient spears she'd seen twice now in her visions, first at the ball when they had pierced McIvor's skull, and second when she'd witnessed the vision while touching Elana.

McIvor was on the floor, kneeling, hands tied in front of him, exactly as he was in Elana's vision.

Elana.

Allegra scanned the room looking for the most likely position she'd find Elana. But she couldn't see any hooded captives. All she saw were bare-chested priests. Two were female, and one male, and neither looked like they were terrified to be there.

McIvor shivered with terror, sweat gleaming on his skin."Wait," he shouted, staring around at the people surrounding him. "You can't do this to me."

The high priest turned to face the ambassador. "Of course we can. You swore your loyalty. You promised your life in payment for any form of betrayal."

"I didn't betray anyone. I'm loyal. I swear. I am. I'm loyal," McIvor shrieked, his voice breaking as terror overcame him.

Allegra shook her head. The scene was the same, exactly as she'd seen it in her vision of Elana's abduction.

McIvor shook his head and stared at one of the women Allegra had considered as possibly Elana. She was tall and slim, her waist tapering in gently, pink nipples hardened and gleaming in the torchlight.

Could *she* be Elana?

Allegra shook her head, unsure of what she was seeing. Logic told her one thing but she couldn't believe it.

"Why?" he cried, his voice plaintive. "Why are you doing this to me?" As Allegra listened she began to understand what was happening.

She heard the grief in his voice and realized that when she'd heard it in Elana's vision, she'd believed he was upset at the high priest for abducting his wife.

He'd been so traumatized and Allegra had believed it was because he feared for his wife's life.

Maybe that was not the case.

On the dais, the high priest began to chant again and Allegra's heart began to race. The green glow of the carving beneath their feet began to throb, growing stronger each passing minute.

Reaching into the dark beyond the sacrificial table, the high priest retrieved the spear Allegra had seen in her vision. Its sharp point glinted all the more dangerously when seeing it in reality.

He lifted the staff, and moonlight reflected on its sharp tip, calling Allegra's attention to the ceiling. In her vision she'd been impressed at the crisscrossing patterns of moonlight, but now it only made her want to throw up.

She watched as the two priests on either side of Elana took her arms and led her forward.

Allegra had felt so much pain for Elana.

A flash of light pulled Allegra back to the scene and she watched as another priest pointed the spear at McIvor's right ear. The man squealed just as he had in her vision, only this time she felt the sound reverberate in her bones.

"We need to do something," Allegra whispered.

"I'll get closer," Athena said, hurrying down the corridor. As she hurried off, Allegra blinked and found herself staring at the hindquarters of a jet-black jaguar.

Movement above her head drew her attention now and she made out the shape of a man silhouetted at one of the windows letting in the moonlight. Narrowing her gaze, she let out a sigh of relief.

The tracker had worked!

Max put a finger to his lips as he produced a coil of climbing rope in his hands. Although Allegra craned her neck to check for backup she found she could only see Max.

He'd come without backup?

She shook her head and ignored him. Perhaps he hadn't been able to obtain support fast enough, but it made no difference now.

She watched below as Elana took the spear from the priest at her side, watched as the high priest drew closer, a sharp short sword in his hand, watched as the Elana raised the weapon and aimed it at her husband's head.

McIvor was quiet now, as if he'd accepted his fate.

The green glow throbbed as Elana pulled the spear back preparing to plunge the deadly sharp point into her husband's head. Pillan was growing stronger, waiting for the sacrifice to be completed, for blood to be spilled so he could walk the mortal earth.

Allegra's heart raced. She had to do something. Allegra grabbed her dagger and without thinking, threw it straight at Elana's raised hand.

At the same time—out of the corner of her eye—she saw the jaguar spring at the high priest, and heard two gunshots followed by a thud in the stone two inches from her face.

She watched as Elana fell to her knees, Allegra's blade embedded deep into the muscles of her forearm, blood from her wound staining her arm and her breasts. She screamed in pain, pulling at the mask and headdress until they fell at her side.

The green glow beneath them flickered and began to fade, and Allegra felt a wave of relief wash over her.

McIvor merely stared at his wife, his eyes flat and emotionless.

Only then did Allegra study the scene. The high priest whose neck was ravaged, his mask askew, the two dead priests beside Elana with bullet-holes in their foreheads, and the rest of the gathering scattering out of the two exits.

And the faded green glow at last sputtering out.

Allegra watched as Max slid down the long rope and landed beside McIvor. Athena appeared at his side, fully clothed now as she spoke quietly in his ear.

Max glanced up and stared at Allegra for a moment before moving around McIvor and looking down at Elana. The woman was still crying but her tears reflected only anger as she spat answers to his questions.

Elana looked up and glared at Allegra, the look sending

shivers down Allegra's spine. Without warning Elana grabbed the hilt of the dagger and pulled hard. She stumbled back with the momentum then steadied herself.

Still holding Allegra's gaze, Elana lifted the knife and, with a defiance and fury that was almost palpable even across the room, she slashed the blade across her neck and slit her throat.

Elana fell to the ground, fresh blood spurting across her breasts, Allegra's dagger clattering on the stone beside her.

The hall faded in Allegra's vision and she gripped the low wall in front of her to steady herself.

She wasn't sure what she'd expected Elana to do, but it wasn't to slit her own throat.

Elana had made her stand, she'd taken the power out of everyone else's hands and killed herself. But Allegra wasn't sure what the woman had hoped to gain from it.

And perhaps that was one thing Allegra would never know. And she was okay with that.

The aftermath was mayhem, but Allegra's heart continued to race as her gaze fell upon the high priest. His mask had shifted, baring more than half his face to her view.

General Qhapaq.

Why was Allegra not surprised?

He'd been behind it all along, been the one who'd wanted to raise a god to the mortal world, had interrogated Allegra to find out if she'd seen anything in her visions that could thwart their grand scheme.

And now he was dead for it.

And so was Pillan, consigned back to whatever realm he lived in. Until of course, some other madman decided to resurrect him.

Humanity was insane.

Allegra scanned the hall for one last face, already knowing she wouldn't see him.

Langcourt had participated in the ritual, and had fled during the mayhem.

And for that Allegra was more disappointed.

Her kidnapper was in the wind again.

CHAPTER 45

*A*llegra took a sip of the chocolate and relaxed against the back of the sofa. She sat on the balcony of their hotel room in Qusqu, staring out at the beautiful blue sky.

The summers here were beautiful and she wished she'd come on a holiday instead of an investigative trip that had turned into something so macabre that she wasn't sure she'd have been able to make it up.

She looked up as Athena entered the room, ushered in by Max who looked about as drained as Allegra felt.

"How are you feeling, my Lady?" Athena asked, smiling softly as she took a seat beside Allegra.

"Sore and tired. You put me through my paces, you know?"

Athena tilted her head and studied Allegra's arms. "You did a very good job. Not many people would have been up to that type of physical exertion even in times of stress."

Allegra shrugged. "I have to thank you, though. For coming to my rescue."

Athena waved a hand. "It's my duty and my pleasure."

"Your duty?"

"Not as Chief Inspector. As a deity of a pantheon that is slowly dying out. I'm a minor demigod, but I still take my responsibility seriously."

"Well, for that I thank you. How did you know I needed help?"

"I've been following you for most of your stay in Qusqu."

Allegra stared, her mouth open. "It was you all along? Outside the embassy and at the ambassador's ball? And the hut above the city when we were on the run?"

Athena nodded. "A good thing too. They abducted you even though you were supposed to be safe. What do you think that means?"

Allegra squinted at the demigod. "They have a mole?"

"Yes. But contrary to what I had originally believed—which was the leak was somewhere within my office—I received information from a reliable source that the mole is too close for comfort."

Allegra's eyebrows rose. She had to admit she was too tired for word games and something in her expression must have told Athena that.

Athena nodded. "Celestra Avesta. She's your mole." When neither Max nor Allegra responded, Athena asked, "Not surprised?"

Allegra shook her head. "Not really. I knew something was going on."

"Well, you'd best get to the bottom of it because she's dangerous." Athena got to her feet.

"That reminds me . . . do we have anything on Langcourt's whereabouts?" Allegra said, giving Max an arch look. He'd been too quiet.

Athena shook her head. "No sign of him. He's disappeared without a trace. I suspect he's left the country by now."

Allegra gritted her teeth at the news, a wave of anger and helplessness running over her. Langcourt had slipped from their grasp again. The man had a nasty way of disappearing on her. Still, she knew more about the man now than she ever wanted to know.

Max got to his feet to show Athena out and Allegra dozed on the sofa until he returned. She wasn't surprised to see he had Les with him.

Allegra was tired, in body and soul. Too tired to even be angry with the woman. Although from the looks of it, Max looked angry enough for the both of them.

"Why did you do it?" Max asked, going straight in for the kill.

Les's spine stiffened. "You don't understand."

"What don't I understand? That you've lied to us, that you'd betrayed us and put Allegra in danger?"

Les shifted her gaze to Allegra her expression apologetic for the briefest moment. Then her eyes hardened. "I wish I could have done otherwise, but believe me when I say I had no choice. And I'd do it again."

Allegra tilted her head and studied Celestra. There was a passion behind her words, a deep sense of purpose even when she sounded conflicted. As if she'd fight to the death for what she protected.

The way a mother would.

The image of a mangled pink teddy bear shimmered in Allegra's vision and her heart stilled.

"I don't care what you say, endangering Allegra is not acceptable." Max had raised his voice, his fury palpable in the room.

"Max?" He glanced over at her, the vein at his temple pulsating.

She didn't respond to his questioning look. Instead she said to Les, "How long have they been holding your child for ransom?"

Max's jaw dropped and Les began to cry as she sank onto the sofa.

"How did you know?" she whispered through her tears.

"The teddy bears in the vision."

Les nodded and began to cry again. Then she cleared her throat. "They've been keeping him for a year now."

CHAPTER 46

Two hours later, Max was on the phone with the extraction team. He'd given them Les's address, having come to the conclusion that since the apartment had been the location of Les's death in Allegra's last vision, that was likely where her little boy was being hidden.

Little Carlo Avesta was two years old and had been taken just under a year ago, and held in order to ensure Les's loyalty. When she'd admitted she hadn't seen or spoken to her boy in all that time, Allegra's stomach had tightened.

But she'd pushed away her fears and waited at Les's side while Max coordinated the rescue mission.

Sitting there in silent horror Allegra had listened as Max relayed the team's progress, as they penetrated the apartment and took down the single guard.

And as they discovered the body of the little boy in the freezer.

Allegra had sat with her arms around Les as the mother grieved for her son. There were no words that could ease her pain. The fact that the captors had killed the child so long ago was clear enough to Les, who was now a shadow of her former self.

Max sent her to bed after she'd calmed down, giving her a low dose tranquilizer while Allegra waited for him to return. There were things they needed to discuss and despite the tragedy, what she had to say couldn't wait.

Max shut the door to the inner room and sighed as he walked over to sit beside Allegra. She felt horrible as she shifted to look at him, knowing she wasn't going to give him any time to de-stress.

"I'll send her to Mara to recuperate."

Allegra nodded. "That's a good idea."

Max tilted his head and studied Allegra's face. "Something you want to talk to me about?"

"Am I that transparent?"

He smiled. "Only because I know you so well."

When Allegra finished her story, bringing Max up to speed on the vision she'd had when she'd touched Langcourt, he sat there for a long moment in total silence.

Then he turned to her and said, "Well . . . that was certainly not what I expected."

Allegra smiled. "Me either."

CHAPTER 47

*H*er vision had faded to nothing. Then, within the blink of an eye, images began to slide across her mind.

Images of a rather stern-looking man, hooded eyes, high cheekbones yet a little soft in the belly. His aristocratic bearing was softened by his enlarged stomach.

More than his physique, his face arrested Allegra's attention. She'd seen that face not so long ago in Londinium. And she'd seen him too in a vision of the past.

At the time, she'd chalked it up to an imagined similarity, but now that she stared at the moving images in the vision, Allegra knew there was more to it than a doppelgänger.

She saw him through time, in places and periods that at first didn't make sense. She'd assumed she was looking at his ancestors, but soon she began to doubt her eyes.

Allegra glared at the man in the vision. As she shifted the image blurred, then focused on something more familiar.

High Priest of the Order of Hermes. Lord Severus Langcourt.

Allegra watched him now, a memory of Delphi, she watched

again as he murdered Cathenna while she felt the very agony of the Pythia's death.

She'd thought Langcourt's bloodline must simply contain a strong gene for physical similarity, but the vision, his memories, pointed to something so much more sinister.

Another set of images showed a small group of four men, all positioning themselves around the body of a dead elephant. They posed, standing around the creature, rifles set on their shoulders, heads held high with pride for their kill.

A thought flitted across her mind, almost as if a memory had filtered through to her. *Lord Alderman Langcourt and sons, 2912.*

Allegra took a shuddering breath. The high priest stood beside the tusk of the elephant, his hand wrapped around the single tusk that remained attached to the poor creature. The other tusk lay on the ground, and another Langcourt stood beside it, one foot set on top of the ivory.

She was caught in the vision, watching image after image fly in front of her, images of Severus Langcourt going back centuries, images or memories of the rest of the family.

Tracking through the memories she focused briefly on one at the time of the Frankia Uprising, images of one other Langcourt had stopped. A member of this—almost immortal—family had likely been killed around that time.

Allegra's heart thudded so hard in her chest that she was a little afraid she would undo whatever healing had taken place since she'd been shot.

She raised a hand and traced the wound, now bare of bandages. Who had it been who'd tried to kill her? Could it have been Langcourt himself?

It was now clear the Langcourts and the Pythian line went back all the way to Delphi before the turn of the century.

But who were these men, this entire family who seemed to possess the gift of immortality? And why did they systematically murder the Pythias through the years.

While they had lived and prospered, the Pythias had been assassinated one after the other.

Langcourt's memories showed so much death among the Pythian line that Allegra was surprised she'd even come to be born at all. This family seemed to have been on an extermination bend that had taken on a resonance of mass murder.

She couldn't believe it, couldn't understand the depth of hatred they must have to have killed so many of her maternal line over two millennia.

EPILOGUE

$\mathcal{M}$ ax stared at the paperwork spread all across Allegra's bed. He'd known Aurelia had left a trunk for the next Pythia but he'd never been made aware of how important it was.

"Do you think this is why Aurelia left the public eye? To keep herself safe here?" Allegra asked softly as she studied a drawing made by a Pythia in the tenth century. The Oracle had used charcoals and colored pollen to create a self-portrait, an act some would say was the height of vanity.

The notes she made were clear enough. She'd wanted her descendants to know what she looked like because she knew that seeing something with one's own eyes cemented that object in a person's consciousness.

"She knew what she was talking about," said Allegra as she stared at the drawing.

"Who is she?"

"Pythia Mirella O'Leary, 2209 to 2247."

"She was so young," Max murmured as he took the drawing.

Allegra sighed. "They killed so many of us," she whispered. A long moment passed in which Max studied the portrait and read the accompanying journal.

"She describes being followed, stalked."

Nodding, Allegra said, "The day before she died she wrote that she was certain something was wrong. She'd been to a social event and she'd felt ill afterward. She wrote that if anything should happen to her it would mean she'd been murdered."

Max shook his head. "This is unbelievable. That a family could decimate an entire lineage. And so systematically."

Allegra frowned, glaring at Max. "Does it not bother you that the current theory is these men are immortal?"

She pointed at the stack of papers, her voice breaking when it went a little too high.

Max smiled. "I know what it sounds like. But there must be some explanation. And if there isn't, then perhaps these men are demigods like Athena Nostrus. If gods are immortal then it stands to reason their progeny would be too."

"You're suddenly very accepting of the existence of the gods."

"I never said I wasn't." Max smiled. "But even if I was, Pienius and Xales are two very good reasons to adjust my perspective."

"So demigods?" Allegra got to her feet and began to pace. She knew she'd be better off sitting and resting, but she felt restless. It was as if she wanted to run out of the room and race across the city, to disappear into the jungle and run until her body gave out.

Max grunted. "Perhaps." After a moment of silence, he said, "Have you ever heard of the Elixir of Immortality?"

Allegra's mouth widened into a grin, and she was about to say it was a myth, and couldn't possibly have any truth to it, but then she closed her mouth.

"Tell me more," was all she said. Who was she to question anything any longer? Her reality had changed when her first vision had hit her. And ever since then it had been changing constantly.

"The Ancient Greeks and the people of Kemet talked about

the existence of magical waters that possessed not only healing properties but the ability to bring the dead back to life as well as to render the user immortal. Only a violent death could kill them. But they would need access to these waters as the power wasn't permanent."

"What about the reanimated people and the diseased? Do their symptoms return eventually too," Allegra asked smiling.

Max pursed his lips as he shook his head. "According to the legend, the waters are healing, so they help the body regenerate what has been diseased, so it healed leprosy and brought the dead back to life. But immortality was a different spectrum. For those who want to live forever, they must partake of the waters every few hundred years. There also were tales of the elixir being carried within the blood of a specific line of people, but that was never corroborated."

"So where exactly was this Elixir to be found? Was it something an alchemist mixed up, or is it waters of the earth" Allegra asked, then scrunched up her face. "Apart from the elixir that runs in some people's veins, that is."

"It was rumored to have come from the source of the River Kemet somewhere in the middle of Lower Kemet."

Allegra sighed. "Unless we go looking for it ourselves, we're unlikely to find it. And besides, what we need to find out is what these men are doing to maintain their longevity. They would be the key, I think. Find out what's keeping them alive and cut off their access to that source."

Max's head shot up and as Allegra stared at the shocked look on his face, the image of a little boy's face shimmered before her, superimposed on Max.

The little boy Langcourt had sacrificed while Allegra had watched, memories Max knew haunted her dreams for long nights afterward.

"Could the child sacrifices have had something to do with Langcourt's desire for extended longevity?"

Allegra nodded. "He was adamant about drinking the blood while it was still warm. In fact, now that I think about it, he was quite agitated toward the end. You think he was using the Cult to help gather the children and then drink their blood fresh from the sacrifice?"

Max's lip curled in a snarl. "When I get my hands on that son of a bitch—"

"You won't be able to do anything to him."

Max huffed and got to his feet. He went to the window and stared out at the view. "This is way too much stress for you. You're supposed to be here to recuperate."

Allegra sighed. "I wish I could recuperate, but there is something else you need to know."

Max's heart jittered as he waited.

She didn't speak. She merely handed him a piece of paper with a name printed on it.

Allegra Jocasta Damaskos.

Which was all fine until he saw the birth date.

A hundred years in the future.

~ TO BE CONTINUED ~

Thank you for reading. The DARK SIGHT Series continues with VISSARION.

FREE STARTER LIBRARY - JOIN MY NEWSLETTER

Get the following titles FREE when you subscribe to my newsletter.

Tee's Newsletter

http://smarturl.it/TeesMailingList

ABOUT THE AUTHOR

I have been a writer from the time I was old enough to recognize that reading was a doorway into my imagination. Poetry was my first foray into the art of the written word. Books were my best friends, my escape, my haven. I am essentially a recluse but this part of my personality is impossible to practice given I have two teenage daughters, who are actually my friends, my tea-makers, my confidantes... I am blessed with a husband who has left me for golf. It's a fair trade as I have left him for writing. We are both passionate supporters of each other's loves – it works wonderfully...

My heart is currently broken in two. One half resides in South Africa where my old roots still remain, and my heart still longs for the endless beaches and the smell of moist soil after a summer downpour. My love for Ma Afrika will never fade. The other half of me has been transplanted to the Land of the Long White Cloud. The land of the Taniwha, beautiful Maraes, and volcanoes. The land of green, pure beauty that truly inspires. And because I am so torn between these two lands – I shall forever remain cross-eyed.

Stalk Tee here:
www.tgayer.com
tee@tgayer.com